Best to
you!

Mick
Peterson

Once A Coach

MICK PETERSON

authorHOUSE®

Cover design by Anthony Easton. Photo courtesy of Catch 'Em In Action Photography.

AuthorHouse™
1663 Liberty Drive, Suite 200
Bloomington, IN 47403
www.authorhouse.com
Phone: 1-800-839-8640

First published by AuthorHouse 11/16/2007

ISBN: 978-1-4343-5037-4 (sc)

Printed in the United States of America
Bloomington, Indiana

This book is printed on acid-free paper.

Acknowledgements

I would like to thank all of my supporters who believed I should tell this story. A special thanks goes to my immediate family, my wife Carole, my daughters Katie, Julie, Emily and my son Drew for allowing me to fulfill two passions- teaching and coaching high school kids- for over thirty-three years. Without their love and encouragement, I would have never had the opportunity to experience this dream of putting all of these wonderful memories to print. I also have to acknowledge all of the coaches, players, and parents whom I worked with over the years for providing me with the material used in this fictional work. Their inspiration has allowed me to present, what I hope to be, a fresh new approach to the greatest game in America, high school football. Finally, I would like to thank my Composition II students at Pontiac Township High School for providing me with their persistence on seeing this project through its completion, with special kudos to Carrie Chandler for her assistance in the compilation of this final manuscript.

This book is dedicated to the memory of my late father, Melvin Peterson, who taught me the meaning of perseverance.

Foreword

I have always believed that high school football has represented the values held dear by Americans - hard work, discipline, camaraderie, persistence, courage, physical and mental toughness, motivation, and leadership, among others. It remains to this day a community event, a chance for partisans of one side to match enthusiasm with those of a heated rival. The aroma of barbecued pork chop sandwiches, the choreography of a finely tuned marching band, and the passion of the cheerleaders and fans can be found in cities and towns all across this great country of ours.

However, behind the color and pageantry lies a human element that so many people don't always see. Whether it's Friday nights or Saturday afternoons, the crowds filling the stands only see the product on display for those two and a half hours. They don't see all of the preparation each week to get to that game. They don't experience what goes on behind-the-scenes in the locker rooms. They don't know that the characters involved in their weekly drama have more to them than a whistle or a helmet.

Once a Coach is based on several real episodes I experienced during my thirty-three years connected with high school football, ten as an assistant coach and the last twenty-three as a head coach. Although the characters in this novel are fictional and the events portrayed here have been formulated, the inspiration for creating the various scenarios came from real people and real happenings. Even though this story is set in the Midwest, it could very easily happen in the hills of Pennsylvania, the vast open land of Texas, the dusty roads of Alabama, or the bluegrass of Kentucky, any place where high school is played.

It is my sincere hope that any coach who has ever worn a whistle, any player who has ever strapped up his helmet, or any fan who has dressed out in school colors will be able to identify with the joys, the pitfalls, and the hope that *Once a Coach* may bring.

Prologue

March 16

Hillsdale is not unlike most Midwestern cities, surrounded by cornfields and rural highways. In the last few years, new "wind farms" have popped up here and there, their gigantic windmill blades gently rolling in circular arcs. For the most part, the city has steadily grown in the past decade. Shopping malls and restaurants dot the outskirts of the city now, engulfing some of the landmark buildings that date back forty, fifty years. One of those "landmarks" was a rickety old diner, known as *The Cabin*.

Even though other more notable eateries were now in Hillsdale, *The Cabin* remained a local favorite. It's really not much different from other greasy spoons around the country, a joint where farmers hung out and talked about the weather and people from all around would come for a fantastic home cooked meal. This restaurant dated back to the forties, the war years, back when the late Elise and Ray Johnson decided to take a chance on a log building they had just constructed at the edge of town. Ray loved to cook steaks, barbecue ribs, and fry chicken, while Elise made the best apple pie anywhere around.

On the outside, people would not think that *The Cabin* would amount to much. Located only two blocks from the high school parking lot, it was still rather small compared to today's standards, with its two modest pillars holding up a broad roof. *The Cabin* still had most of the original booths in place Ray put in back in the fifties. It only had to be upgraded once during that time, back in the mid-seventies, after a small fire broke out in the kitchen when Elise tripped and spilled some hot grease from the chicken fryer. Nobody got hurt, and Ray and Elise both laughed about it later. She said that was the only way she could get Ray to spend some money on the place. Their picture still hangs right behind the cash register.

"*The Cab*," as the kids today called it, never seemed to have an empty parking lot. Breakfast, lunch, or dinner- it never mattered; customers would face all kinds of weather at all hours of the day, especially after Hillsdale High School sporting events. The menu had evolved somewhat, but the food was still that good. The flashing lights from the rooftop could be seen all the way across town. In over sixty years, *The Cabin* had plenty of stories to tell. That raw, March night would be no different.

The door opened, and a tall male stood under the awning for a moment.

"Sometimes," he thought, as he zipped his Gortex jacket snugly around his neck, "the weather around here does match the mood of the moment."

A cold, damp rain splattered the face of the dark figure as he headed out to his truck. Underneath his jacket, he held his laptop securely, protecting it from the elements. As he crawled into the 2000 Ford, Coach Ben Reynolds let the water dribble down his nose for a second.

What he figured to be a good idea earlier that evening had really turned out to be a bummer. He thought the lady would have been impressed with his little DVD, but it appeared she could have cared less. She seemed to be more interested in whether her son could join various clubs. That's not what he had thought when he first came.

In fact, he never really wanted to come at all to *The Cabin* to begin with that night. However, when the Norton family had called him initially, they seemed to be decent people. All they had wanted to do was talk about the Hillsdale schools because they were moving to town. This wasn't Reynolds' area of expertise, but they insisted on seeing him specifically. They had heard he was a guy who would "shoot straight."

It didn't matter to Reynolds that the Nortons had a son who was supposed to be a good football player. During his 15-year tenure at Hillsdale, the coach had heard that claim from virtually every move-in he had ever encountered.

No, what bothered him was the fact that Mrs. Norton was concerned that her son would only be "just a number" at the school, "not a person." Since they were coming from a smaller community, she wondered whether people in Hillsdale actually cared about each other.

Despite his insistence to the contrary, Mrs. Norton wasn't convinced over the phone. Actually, that was another thing that perturbed Reynolds. She never got on the phone herself. Instead, she had her husband, a really nice guy, do the talking while she lurked in the background, chirping in whenever she felt it necessary and having her husband repeat what she said.

Obviously, the Nortons weren't familiar with the Hillsdale "family." Coach Reynolds had gone to great lengths to make family and community a vital part of his football program. Last fall, in fact, he had produced a DVD honoring the mothers of the senior class. It had been his daughter Jo Ellen's idea. He used pictures and video clips from the players' childhood he had collected, mixed in some video highlights from the past season, added Senior Night photos with players and moms, and then put it all to music. It wasn't Steven Spielberg or anything, but when he had shown it at the banquet, there wasn't a dry eye in the place. Hillsdale people care; there's no doubt about it.

That's why Reynolds had agreed to meet this family at Hillsdale's favorite restaurant and also why he brought his laptop. He decided to "prove" his point to Mrs. Norton. When he popped the DVD in, he just knew in his heart the two Nortons would understand and appreciate the message, just like all of the Hillsdale people had. Just thirty seconds in, though, and the lady was looking at her notes. Dad seemed to like it, but it could have just been respect for the situation. Reynolds didn't recall if the boy was watching or not. In fact, that kid really didn't say much of anything the whole time they were in there. Big deal! What a waste of time!

As Reynolds started his truck, he noticed the family scurrying to their SUV. He had told them if they wanted particular information about the school, they needed to contact Mrs. Smythe, the school counselor and Mr. Hubbard, the school principal as soon as possible, if they were really interested. He wondered if they would or not, but then shrugged his shoulders. Big deal!

He shifted gears and began to leave the parking lot. "What was the boy's name?" he said to himself. "Jerry? Jimmy? Joey?" He chuckled at his lack of perception.

He looked at his watch. 7:50. Just enough time to get home to watch *24*. "Some things are more important than others," he thought, as he sped down the road.

"Oh, yeah." It then came to him. "His name's Jack." Just like Jack Bauer. He felt better knowing he hadn't totally lost his mind.

The rain continued to fall as the truck disappeared into the night, the lights atop the roof of *The Cabin* still flashing.

Part 1

July 15

Chapter 1

"Huh, humph, huh, humph, huh, humph."

The heavy breathing from the morning run was all that could be heard down the street. These daily early workouts had begun as a means to an end for Jeff Fairchild earlier this summer. He felt the only way he could earn playing time his final year was to do something drastic, something that nobody else was willing to do. So, in addition to the weight training, conditioning, and team throwing drills he had religiously attended all summer for the Hillsdale Hillmen, Jeff had decided to get up at dawn and go for a run each day. Sundays too. He had been doing these runs since June 2, the last day of school.

At first, they weren't long runs, but they were strenuous, especially for a guy who really never liked running. As he began to build up endurance ("Why didn't I run track this spring?" he wondered early on in his training) and added some distance to them, they actually had become fun. Of course, listening to his favorite country music on his Ipod helped take his mind off the work at hand.

1

Jeff Fairchild never had to be told twice what to do. Since his dad had died prematurely two years ago from a sudden heart attack, he had been forced to grow up a great deal. It had always been his dad's dream to see his son get to play for Hillsdale's varsity, just like he had done some twenty years earlier, but that was no longer a reality. Instead, Jeff had taken on several "man of the house' duties. Besides helping his mom whenever he could and keeping a part-time job at "The Cabin," Jeff had also earned some money mowing lawns and helping tutor his little neighbor friend Ricky with math over the summer. But wearing that uniform and playing under the lights on Friday nights…. that's what Jeff really wanted to do.

Jeff wasn't stupid, either. He knew he didn't have the talent of some of the other kids on the team. He wasn't as fast as Jake Lewis, or as strong as Matt Gerard, or as good a blocker as Mitch Lupinski. He was somewhere in between all of those guys. So he knew he was going to have to do a little more, if he expected to get any kind of a shot.

He always heard his father's words echoing through his mind. "If you want something bad enough, you're going to have to work to earn it. Nothing is ever given to a Fairchild," his dad had said numerous times. He would be ready, just like his longtime idol "Rudy" from Notre Dame fame. He even liked the fact the other guys called him "Rudy." That meant he belonged; he was respected

What he didn't like was that Brad Brown was not going to be there this year, however. It had been three months since Brad's dad up and took him out of school and moved him to Valley Forge, of all places. Valley Forge was going to be the opening game this fall, just like it had been the past seven years. The two towns had built up quite a little rivalry during that time.

Brad would have been Hillsdale's starting running back. He had all of the physical tools Jeff wished that he possessed. The word on the street was that Brad's dad didn't like Coach Reynolds. Jeff couldn't really get that. Coach had always seemed fair. It just didn't make any sense. But then again, Jeff really didn't worry about stuff like that. He already had enough on his plate.

Jeff turned the corner and began to stride out a little bit longer. Four miles and counting, and Toby Keith had never sounded better. He looked up and, sure enough, there was Coach Reynolds out for his morning walk with his beagle Champ. Jeff often saw the coach in the morning, but he rarely stopped to talk. He didn't want to make it look like he was sucking up.

On this morning, he waved, though. "Hi Coach!" and put his head down for the final push. He had lawns to mow today.

July 15

Chapter 2

Jason Stone tapped his finger on his laptop nervously. He had been working for the State Athletic Association for over one month, and the only real job he had to do thus far was organize the starting dates for fall practices and put them on the State web site. That, and update the file on open dates for all sports. Not busy work, mind you, but close to it.

He knew that, despite graduating from college with honors, he had gotten this job as a favor to his uncle. Everybody in the state had heard of Randy Stone, the best statistical baseball player ever seen in the Midwest and currently the starting catcher for the Cubs. As Uncle Randy had told him often growing up, "Son (*Jason hated that word*)…it's not always *what* you know; it's *who* you know that counts."

Jason had never been one to back down from a challenge. He remembered a time in high school that he stayed in the batting cage after practice for thirty extra minutes one day after his baseball coach had told him, "Randy Stone would stay up to an hour a day after everybody else for extra hitting." That was the difference, though. Uncle Randy would do it every day; Jason only did it just that once.

Jason looked at his watch. 7:50 AM. He took pride in that he was always punctual for appointments. Maybe this meeting with Mr. Phillips, the State Director, would be something important, a chance to make his own name for himself. Maybe it would be a big project that would earn him respect around the office. The tapping now had a rhythm.

Jason really couldn't figure out Monty Phillips. Phillips had only taken over as the head man in January, and most of the same problems coaches had been complaining about in the past still existed. Playoffs. Media coverage. More classes. Fewer classes. Eligibility issues. Fewer quality referees. The only good thing Stone knew had come out of the first six months is that everybody on staff who wanted one could get a free membership at the nearby country club.

That, plus new laptops for the staff and the offices all got painted. Not much else had happened. Jason did remember reading in the paper just a couple of weeks ago that the State decided to sign a contract with *Wilson Sporting Goods*, so that all of the state series would use *Wilson* balls. Amazing that he didn't hear about it around the office first. That was Phillips' way sometime, he was told.

Phillips was rarely seen around the complex. He was in the building all right, but most of the communications staff received came via e-mail. But nobody could really get a read on him at all, the type of person he was, his likes and dislikes. He had been friendly during Jason's interview, but he mainly just sat there while his assistant Tom Thomas ran the show. He truly was a tough man to read.

Jason looked at his computer screen one more time. "Be in my office at 8 tomorrow morning. M. Phillips." He got up and walked toward the door, fixing his tie one last time. He stopped by the water fountain and took a sip. It made his throat feel better.

He paused one last time before Phillips' door, barely acknowledging Judy Watson, the administrative secretary, took a deep breath, and looked at his watch. 8:00. He knocked. Why were his hands sweaty?

"Come in, Jason."

Stone opened the door and Monty Phillips was sitting behind his desk, coat off, tie unloosened. It was apparent that he had been there for awhile.

"Jason, I got a phone call I want you to check into."

July 15

Chapter 3

Banging on the window air conditioner seemed to help. The "grinding" sound his son had told him about was gone.

William "Bubba" Brown sat at the kitchen counter, his eyes wandering around this Spartan three-room apartment he and his son now called "home" in Valley Forge. The last three months had been hard on him and his family, but he knew he had made the right choice; they had to get out of Hillsdale. That Reynolds guy was an ass!

It didn't matter where they had gone, but Brad was never going to get a scholarship playing for that fricking idiot. That man had no clue how to handle kids, parents, or anybody. All he knew was how to screw over families…. and potentially great players.

Bubba sipped his coffee. It was pretty strong. He had been up since 6:00, and he was on his second pot. It was about time to get Brad up for morning workouts. Now that summer was half over, Bubba had started to get excited a little. The regular season was only a month or so away from starting, and people in Valley Forge would start to know just how good Brad Brown is.

He looked at his son sleeping on the make-shift bed in the other room. The boy never said much; he just went about his business day after day. Bubba had noticed Brad actually had a little chip on his shoulder lately. When he asked him about matters, though, all Brad would say, "It's okay." That's about all Brad ever said to his father.

It hadn't been okay when they first moved out of town. Brad had wanted to stay for his senior year with his buddies; who could blame him? "You'll thank me in the long run, son," Bubba had said more than once, but their relationship had become estranged at best. Although his son complied with his father's wishes, Brad seldom spoke

Until recently. In the past ten days, Brad had begun to bring a couple of friends over. They never stayed long; there wasn't enough room, and Bubba couldn't keep enough food in the refrigerator long enough to feed those kids. Well, at least Brad was smiling when he brought those guys over. He still didn't say a whole lot, but he looked like he was having a good time.

So Brad was somewhere between the chip and the grin, Bubba thought. The boy tossed a bit in his sleep.

He thought about calling his wife Helen back in Hillsdale. He knew she would be getting up soon to go to work. They had never sold their house there because there was no way the family would permanently live in a town like Valley Forge. Once Brad got through with football, got that scholarship, and then graduated, Bubba was going to get rid of this dump of an apartment and they would move on from there. Where that would be he hadn't decided yet.

It didn't matter that both he and his wife seldom saw each other during the week. Half the time she was working and he stayed with Brad; the other half he would work while Helen came to Valley Forge. They had been lucky that the warehouse they both worked at let them do this. Of course, the story they both used about an invalid mother in hospice didn't hurt, either.

It didn't matter that he couldn't cook very well either. Brad had turned out to be a pretty good chef on his own. Spaghetti and macaroni and cheese were his specialties.

It also didn't matter that he was driving that beat-up old Chevy ½ ton he picked up at the used car lot. It just didn't matter. They would show Reynolds. They would show that asshole.

"Brad! Brad! Time to get up, boy."

The sun was shining, and it was going to be hot. A great day to get better.

July 15

Chapter 4

"Hi, Jeff!" Coach Reynolds actually smiled at the boy as he ran by. "What a great kid," he thought. "Too bad he doesn't have the talent to match his heart."

"Champ," Reynolds said, "you may be faster than that young man." The dog seemed to be more intent on sniffing for something in the grass.

Ben Reynolds knew, though, that it was kids like Jeff Fairchild who made coaching still enjoyable to him, even after thirty years in the business. His greatest thrill was to see kids like Jeff make something of themselves, both in athletics and, more importantly, in life after they graduate. He especially thought it special if he and his family were invited to a former player's graduation party or, better yet, his wedding. Those events seemed to make all the hours, all the stress, and all the anxiety worth it.

Walking slowly down a street he had visited virtually every day since they got Champ a year ago, Reynolds decided today was just as good as any to start thinking about what lay down the road. Today was his fiftieth birthday, and his wife Julie wanted to have a little spread that evening. Ben himself really didn't like to host parties all that much, but today was different. He actually was looking forward to it.

Fifty. I'm fifty. How many more years can I do this? How many more years do I want to? How many more practices? He knew he had started to lose some weight, and, whenever he brushed his hair in the morning, he noticed that there was less to worry about. How many more bus rides? How many more parents? How many more derelicts? How many more Bubba Browns are out there?

Despite the high temperature of this July morning, Ben shivered as he thought once again of that April morning when Bubba Brown stormed into his office, knocking over chairs, a memory that just kept coming back over and over in his head these days. It had been hard to stay calm during the ensuing tirade.

"You don't know crap about football! You don't know crap!" Brown had screamed. "My kid isn't good enough to be captain? You don't know shit!"

"The kids voted; all I did was count the ballots." Trying to reason with that lunatic was fruitless; it was then and it probably hadn't changed since.

"If you're the coach, you can name who you want! My boy's the best! He deserves it!" Brown was getting hoarse.

"Sorry. Our team players vote. That's the way it's always been." Reynolds had felt his blood pressure rising. He had begun to edge toward Brown. His right hand clenched into a fist.

"You suck, you sonvabitch! I'll fix you!" Brown rasped toward him, waving his finger. "You'll know who Brad Brown is, you asshole." With that, he stormed out of the room, slamming the door after him. He knocked down two benches for extra effect as he left the locker room.

Three days later, Brad Brown transferred to Valley Forge.

It was episodes like that which lingered in Ben Reynolds' mind. It bothered him that this single occurrence wouldn't go away. Rather than count the number of blessings kids like Jeff Fairchild brought to the table, it was the frickin' idiots like Bubba Brown who left scars on his psyche.

Despite always complaining to his wife about being the only one who got this dog-duty, Ben was actually beginning to enjoy these morning walks. They gave him time to clear his head. Today was no different. As Champ lurched to chase a white-tailed squirrel, Ben squeezed the handle of the leash. "Hey, Champ! Settle down!"

He knew he needed to as well. Settle down, that is. The game of football had been very good to him, and he felt he had tried to give just as much back to the game. Hillsdale's reputation had grown greatly during his tenure. After fifteen years at the helm, his Hillmen had won ten conference championships, with another twelve trips to the State tournament. However, no state titles had come the Hillmen way... They had come close a couple of times; most recently last year, losing a heartbreaker in the closing minutes of the semi-final game.

Like most coaches, Ben Reynolds agonized over those gut-wrenching losses much more than celebrating the numerous wins. That type of frustration ate at him, but he never publicly let on. He always wondered afterwards, though, what else could he, the coach, have done to change things? Most of the time, no answer came. That last November crusher had bothered him almost all the way to Christmas. Julie had spent most of December trying to cheer him up.

He could still see the ball slipping through Brad Brown's fingers inside the five-yard line. Brown probably would have scored, but we'll never know. That fumble with less than a minute to go sealed the Hillmen's doom. A three point loss to Mt. Carroll, who ended up winning it all a week later.

He recalled how long Brad had sat on the floor of the locker room after the game, just staring into space, with his muddied uniform still on. No matter what anybody tried to say, the young man could not be consoled. Bubba had waited outside for almost an hour for his son to finally clean up and go home.

Reynolds felt a tug on his socks. Champ's wagging tail and sparkly eyes told him it was time to go home. Breakfast would be ready. Biscuits and gravy. Julie only made that on special occasions. Like today. He was fifty.

And, then, all of a sudden, just like Forrest Gump, one of his many fictional heroes, he then decided that this was going to be his last year. Like Forrest said, when he began his three year run, "No apparent reason." Just like that. It was time. "Happy birthday to me," he whistled as he and Champ strolled down the street to his house.

July 15

Chapter 5

Tom Hallion was tired. Working midnights and then coming home to update this new computer website concoction he had developed the past three weeks had begun to take its toll. The fact that he was single with no ties to anyone excused the four days of not shaving. He rubbed the stubble as he sat down to work on his new web site, "Rocco's Rocks."

It was a weird name for a high school football website, but Hallion didn't feel it was any worse that some of the others he had seen from elsewhere around the state. Ones like "Pigskin Pointers" and "High School Gridiron Groupies" or, his personal favorite, "Helmet Honkers." He knew that none of those really paid much attention to the schools around here; they were much more involved with the bigger city schools. Yet, anyone who followed high school football closely knew that this central part of the state was known for the toughness of its players, the caliber of its coaches, and the rabid nature of the fans who came to the games.

He ought to know; he was once one of them. Hallion had played at Northtown back about ten years ago. He was an OK player in his day, by his own admission, nothing to write home about, but not too shabby. He was an All-Conference defensive back who also did the kicking for Northtown. Hallion knew his stats, too. All you had to do was ask him. Forty-seven tackles his senior year, five interceptions and two fumble recoveries. He would have run one of those picks back for a touchdown but he tripped over his own feet as he tried to jitter-bug step and fell at the eight yard line. Twenty for twenty on PAT kicks with a three for four in field goal tries, his longest from 40 yards. He also knew the wind conditions for each of those kicks (the 40-yarder was into the wind), plus the down and distance, plus the name of the quarterback on each of his interceptions.

Yes, Hallion was a football junkie. He had forgotten more than most people knew about The Sky Conference schools and their football rivalries. He knew the score from the first Northtown-Hillsdale football game, played way back in 1901. He knew the name of the coaches involved in the highest scoring game in the history of the conference. He knew each of the coaches in the conference today pretty well, but he especially liked Ben Reynolds, the guy from Hillsdale. That guy knew what he was doing, both on and off the field.

He also had heard about that Brown fellow and his son. With only little more a month to go before Opening

Day, that game between Hillsdale and VF looked like it might be a fun one. Lots of comments popped up as people on his site were starting to get lathered a bit.

"Let's see who has something intelligent to say," he muttered to himself. "Or better yet, something stupid."

July 15

Chapter 6

She reached for the bottle on the bottom shelf. Time for her daily dose. The doctor had told her these pills would help calm her nerves, but Julie Reynolds really had only seen a little change in her behavior. Mostly, the pills served as a placebo, and she really took them only to make her husband happy.

Julie Reynolds appeared to most to be the perfect coach's wife. A high school cheerleader herself and daughter of a coach, she understood the peaks and valleys her husband experienced each and every year. However, behind the smiling face and seemingly happy-go-lucky attitude, Julie struggled to separate the downers from the successes. Recently, she had begun crying for no reason. Well, she knew the reason…she hadn't recovered from the Brown incident.

The Hillsdale community loved her. She was active in the school's boosters club, the United Way, as well as her church ladies' group. In the past ten years, she had earned everyone's respect as a top real estate agent, going "Gold" four years in a row. At games, she was always decked out in school colors, and everyone heard her cow bell. She knew that most of the fans were in Ben's corner, so she tried to tune out those who openly questioned his calls. Once in awhile, she couldn't resist.

During a game a few years ago, one of the juniors' dads yelled out, "C'mon coach! Put somebody in who can block!" Julie quickly retorted, "He's waiting 'til the second half!" Everybody heard her, and the dad sat down.

But she knew that Ben was naïve. Either that or he was oblivious to what's going on or he just didn't care. Her feisty Irish background refused to let any outsider trod on any of her family. Ben always just tried to shrug any of those episodes off. "No big deal!" he always would say.

It didn't take long for word about Bubba Brown to get around town. Julie heard the whispers. Or at least, she felt a little temperature drop with some of the people she met. She could see that they were aware, but didn't really know what to say, making for an uncomfortable feeling. Ben had been visibly upset when he came home that night. The principal had even called him in. Hubbard wanted to know if Brown had been right about the team captains and how they were selected. That's when Julie lost it. She wanted to go down to Hubbard's office the next day and beat the crap out of him. Enough was enough! That's when the pills started. Doctor Huff said they would help keep her relaxed.

She was hoping, deep down inside, that Ben would think about retiring. He had aged, in the past five years, especially. More gray hair and wrinkles, along with a little weight loss, had slowly crept in on her husband. He was still a handsome man, and he still had a solid build, but he just didn't have that spring in his step like he used to. "I wonder," she thought, "if he still really loves it."

She would never say anything to him about it. That decision would have to come from him. She understood the male ego.

That's why she planned this party. Julie felt that getting Ben surrounded by some of his close friends would jumpstart him into this season. In the fifteen years at Hillsdale, the Reynolds' had developed a pretty tight-knit group of people to lean on. They could get Ben going pretty easily. What better way than on his 50th birthday!

"Oh," she snapped back to her work. "I almost forgot. The biscuits are almost ready."

She looked up and saw Ben and Champ strolling down the street. He appeared to be whistling. A smile came to her face. Maybe the pill was working, after all.

July 15

Chapter 7

"A phone call!" Jason had initially thought. That had been his knee-jerk reaction. All this anxiety over a stupid phone call!

Once Monty Phillips had explained things to him, though, it sounded like more than just an ordinary phone conversation. This could be the break he was looking for.

When Jason walked out of the office, he had a REAL job to do, investigate a potential recruiting violation. Now, he had heard of private schools getting accused of recruiting, but it was a rare occasion for a public school to be involved. Phillips had explained that he had received four or five of these calls since January, and, like the ones before, he didn't think this one would amount to much either. Jason thought that Phillips just didn't want to be bothered with it.

For Stone, on the other hand, this was virgin territory.... and an opportunity. He was determined to make this performance a quality effort. He had spent the last half hour or so reading the State Athletic Manual, making sure he thoroughly comprehended the recruiting scene. He had to know all of the ins and outs if he was going to sound as if he knew what he was talking about when he contacted…what was the name of that school again?

He looked down at his notes, which now had stretched to three pages. "Willow something," he muttered. "Willow… Willow…Willow Brook. That's it!"

He decided to look up Willow Brook on the web to learn as much as he could before making contact. "Let's see. Class 1A….200 students…AD's name….Ted Morgand. Okay, a little school with a big problem. I've never heard of this place. Let's see where it is " He clicked on Mapsearch. "About 60 miles away. About 15 miles from Hillsdale. OK."

He spun his chair back around and began to hit the buttons.

A few seconds later, he swallowed. "Good morning. My name is Jason Stone, from the State Athletic Association….."

July 15

Chapter 8

The workout was about over. After an hour in the weight room, the Warriors of the Valley Forge varsity were now finishing their thirty minutes outside by running the bleachers in figure 8s.

Bubba sat in his Chevy truck, just like he did every other workout, windows down, leaning on the edge of the window, squinting into the morning sun. The truck itself was not much to look at, with its rusty running board and no hubcaps on the tires. The grille had lost a couple of pieces in the front, and there was no tailgate.

Bubba never got out of the truck for a closer look. While the boys were inside lifting, he would read the morning paper and do the crossword puzzle. He wasn't smart enough to do the Sudoku puzzle, but he enjoyed the challenge the crossword brought. But, when the boys came outside for conditioning, the paper was folded on the seat, and Bubba would stare intently at what was happening.

From what he could see, today looked to be a good day for Brad in the sprints. He won all four of the forty-yard dashes and four of the five sixty-yarders. He seemed to have a little extra burst this morning.

It also sure didn't hurt that Coach Buchanan was doing the timing today. Jim Buchanan was a big man, a robust 6-4, 235 lbs., and, when the weather was hot, he always came to workouts wearing his "wife-beater" white tank-top. He had been a former College All-American, and he commanded respect from everyone. In some ways, he was intimidating, especially when his deep voice echoed on the field. Bubba was a little afraid of him himself; that's why he stayed in the truck all the time. He didn't want to get in the way or get yelled at.

Buchanan was just the type of coach Brad needs, Bubba thought. He remembered what the Coach had shown the two of them the first day Bubba had brought Brad to the office. He had pointed to a huge chart on the wall. "Look here, this is the list of all my players who have gone to play college football. Forty-three in twenty years of coaching. The ones in capital letters…those 12 got D-1 Scholarships. You want a scholarship? You came to the right place," Buchanan had said.

The workout was over. Coach Buchanan called Brad over and put both arms on Brad's shoulders, said something quickly, and patted him on the backside. Brad slowly began the walk towards Bubba's truck.

Bubba pulled down the visor right in front of him. On it was taped an old faded photo of Coach Ben Reynolds.

Brown never missed a chance to sneer at the picture. "See, asshole!" he snarled. "You don't have a clue."

Brad was right outside the truck.

"What'd he want?"

"Who?"

"Coach Buchanan."

"He said to get my head out of my ass. He said I needed to get faster."

"Faster? You won practically every sprint!"

"Not good enough for him. In fact, he called me slow."

"How fast were you?"

"4.8. I can do better."

Bubba looked at Reynolds's picture again and smiled his toothless grin. Then he spit on Reynolds' image.

July 15

Chapter 9

The party had gone on better than Julie could have imagined. It just wasn't the gifts; and it just wasn't the food; and it just wasn't the surprisingly pleasant July evening. It was Ben.

All night long, he had been beaming. She hadn't seen that look on his face in a long time, maybe since the last time the family had gone on vacation over three years ago. She always knew the best way to make Ben smile was to either make him an apple pie or get him near the ocean. Three years ago, the whole Reynolds family, Ben and his family of four, his brother Ryan and his family of six, and his sister Mary and her family of five, had all migrated to Hilton Head for some golf and beach life. No worries. No parents. No football. They just had a fabulous, relaxing, fun time, especially the night the resort held a "Karaoke Night." Ben, Ryan, and Mary joined forces to sing their version of "Dancing Queen." People were rolling in the aisles, laughing.

Julie hadn't seen that glimmer in Ben's eyes since then. They hadn't even gone on vacation the past two years. They had sent their two twin children, Tommy and JoEllen, to different sports camps while they had been in high school, but football just seemed to be monopolizing more and more time.

Once the dishes were cleared and the cackling and insults from the presents had died down, Ben called everyone together.

"We need to do things like this more often, you know that?" he said. "When was the last time any of us has laughed this hard?"

"When was the last time you turned 50?" It was Jerry Smith, Ben's top assistant. Everybody snickered.

"No, I mean it," Ben continued. "I can't think of when I've had so much fun. Maybe when my family had a reunion a few years back. But nothing like that since."

"Okay, where's the party next week? Jerry, how about your place?" Julie felt she should chime in.

Jerry just lifted his glass and nodded.

Ben wasn't finished. "You know, I've been doing some thinking. I've been coaching a long time. Lots of hours. Too many hours, sometimes, I think. I've forgotten just how much I can have. So, I think, after this year, I'm gonna let someone else be the head coach."

"You what?"

"Are you crazy?"

"You frickin' lost it?"

"Have you lost your mind?"

"What is wrong with you?"

"You'll never do it!"

"Oh, yeah, I will. You'll see," Reynolds retorted after the last exchange. " Let me tell you something. Coaching today is a grind. You guys know that. It's a 365 day, 24 hours a day grind. It's not like the old days, back when I started, when all we did was worry about the 4 week pre-season and then the regular season. Now we have off-season weight training, spring conditioning, summer camps, summer workouts, passing tournaments, Linemen's Challenges, pre-season, regular season, before school and after school practices, playoffs, and banquets. And that's only some of it. I've been doing this for over twenty years. It's time to let someone else...someone like Jerry here...to get a chance to do it."

Jerry dropped his drink on the floor. He quickly tried to clean it up with a napkin.

"What'll you do, Ben?" asked Kurt Hayes, one of his good friends.

"I'm not sure, yet, but I know I'm doing the right thing. Look, I may be just fifty, but I'm not a spring chicken. The knees have been acting up, and my back has been sore for awhile. The body doesn't lie, guys; the body doesn't lie." Ben was surprised at how calm and relaxed he was.

Despite their efforts to change his mind, Ben remained firm. So, after about twenty minutes of arguing and attempts at persuading, Kurt suggested they should have a toast. In fact, they had several toasts. One more year. A good group of kids to go out with. That way, he was going to be able to walk away from coaching on *his* terms, nobody else's. Julie knew that was his male ego filtering through.

Once everyone had left, Ben walked back into the kitchen where Julie was at the sink, finishing the last bit of dishes. He slowly crept up behind her and hugged her around the waist. As he gave her a big squeeze, he said, "You're not disappointed, are you?"

She spun around and looked into his eyes, tears welling in her own. She shook her head. "No, not all. Look, I'll show you how disappointed." She picked the bottle of pills and tossed them into the garbage can. They came together once more and just stood in the middle of the kitchen floor for what seemed to be an eternity. He slowly petted her neck, something he had started to do back when they were dating many years ago. They really couldn't tell if it was relief, joy, or ecstasy. But they were both happy, for the first time in a long while.

Ben broke away first. "I'm heading to bed, honey. See you upstairs." He kissed her on the cheek and slowly moved away. As he headed towards the staircase, he noticed that their house phone had a message on it. He checked the dial and noticed it had come from the high school office at 5:00 that afternoon.

"That's weird. Who would be at the school that late today?" he wondered as he accessed the voice mail.

"Ben, this is Alton Hubbard. I need to see you in my office tomorrow morning at 8. We may have a problem."

"Oh, brother," Ben said as he hung up the phone and trudged up the stairs. "Now, what kid will this be about?"

Julie Reynolds didn't hear him. She sniffed and wiped her eyes at the sink. She couldn't wipe the smile off her face, however.

Part 2

July 25

Chapter 10

Rumors! For the most part, Tom Hallion hated rumors. Most of them emerged through the jealousy of crazy fans or, even worse, psycho parents. Very few of them had any merit whatsoever.

On the other hand, his web site dealt with rumors. People who signed in on the "Rocco's Rocks" lived for them. Hit after hit would relay this tidbit of information or that piece of statistic; most of them were, in Tim's eyes, "incoherent babble." Yet, he knew that it was up to him to check up on each of these innuendos, for several reasons. First, he would squelch the slanderous attack by not even allowing one to reach the site. Next, he would refute the obvious fallacy by relaying the proper truthful information. Then, he would investigate the questionable and provide guidance and truth as he could get it to his readers. Finally, he would substantiate the truth by not only verifying what was being presented, but he would also add whatever bonus pieces of information he could.

Even though he had to censor sometimes up to twenty hits per day, Tim knew that this was the only way for this site to make money. These were high school fans talking to other high school fans, or, more importantly, sometimes talking directly to him about the greatest subject in the world…the game of football.

So as the season was drawing even closer, the hits were becoming extremely numerous; over 150 had been posted since he last checked a couple of hours ago. Most of them had to do with a story coming out of Hillsdale. Folks were saying that Coach Ben Reynolds was in trouble for recruiting a kid from Willow Brook.

Tim's first reaction when he saw the story was total rejection and disbelief. Of all the coaches in the area, he liked Coach Reynolds the best. Coach had been in Hillsdale a long time and seemed to run a top-notch, clean, well-respected program. His teams always played hard and did things right. Tim remembered the fiasco from the spring when that Brown nut up and moved his kid to Valley Forge. His site got lots of hits on that; over 90% were in Coach Reynolds' corner. Tim also knew that Brad Brown was a good player, not great, at least not yet. Playing for VF this fall would be quite interesting, especially with that maniac Jim Buchanan calling the shots.

What was really confusing about this story from Hillsdale is why a Hillsdale coach would waste his time on a player from Willow Brook. That town hadn't produced a quality football player in years. They hadn't had a winning season since 1999, and before that, only three winners in the past twenty years.

So, was this true, or was it a hoax? Was Bubba Brown behind it, as some posters argued? After all, he's goofy enough to try and set Coach Reynolds up. Tim felt he couldn't ignore this issue, because it was just too weird. So, he quit typing and decided to make a few phone calls.

July 25

Chapter 11

Jason Stone had set his cruise at 72 as he motored down the highway to Hillsdale. This was a huge moment for him, although he really didn't think the trip was going to amount to much. Information he had gathered in the past week was sketchy at best, and, as he looked at it and evaluated it, it appeared to look more and more like "sour grapes."

The most important thing to him was that he continue to make a solid first impression. He felt confident that he looked the part today. Stone took pride in his wardrobe. Dockers, Hilfiger, and Brookstone shoes or nothing, as far as he was concerned. His hair was styled just like he wanted it, short, cropped with no excess in any area. Stone was one of those rare males who actually enjoyed pedicures, manicures, and tanning beds. It never hurt to look good.

His workout regimen was well-known at the office, even though he had only been there just over a month. Free weights on Monday, machines on Wednesday, a combo on Friday. One hour was all that he needed to complete his workout at the fitness center. Stone ran on Tuesdays and Thursdays, early mornings before he came to work. Some at the office felt he just was trying to make an impression; in a way, they were right. Stone had been taught at an early age that people will respect an individual who presents a solid image. That he would always try to do.

This was his first "investigation," and he felt it would amount to little more than a few questions and maybe a slap on the wrist. He really didn't think the allegations facing Hillsdale had much merit. No, in Stone's mind, the important thing for him this day would be to handle himself well "in the arena" and impress Tom Thomas, the man who had originally hired him and who sat next to him now in the company SUV.

Thomas sat quietly, reading through the material Jason had provided him. Ever since he had first left Phillips' office, Stone had spent most of his waking hours trying to learn as much as he could about Willow Brook, Hillsdale, Coach Ben Reynolds and the Norton family. The first three had been relatively easy, but the Nortons, now, they had presented a challenge. In fact, he had used most of his time gathering material about this quiet family from tiny Willow Brook. There just wasn't much to learn.

William and Priscilla Norton and their son Jack lived in a small two bedroom bungalow close to the Baptist church where William was the pastor. They chose not to live in the parsonage for some unknown reason; nothing Stone could learn indicated anything out of the ordinary regarding the reason for their decision. Priscilla, a teacher herself at one time, did not feel, apparently, that the Willow Brook school system provided enough of a background to give her son enough of an academic challenge. Thus, she felt he wouldn't be able to compete at the college level. It was her idea to move to a bigger, more intense school district, and Hillsdale seemed to fit the bill.

Jack had some ability, Stone learned, both in the classroom and in the athletic arena. As a student, he was gifted, especially with the less than challenging curriculum Willow Brook offered. At 6' 2" and 200 lbs., the young man possessed enough talent that his father thought could be monopolized at a bigger school. At Willow Brook, a school with little or no tradition in any sport, William didn't feel his son would get any looks from any type of college scouts in either baseball or football. The boy, for his part, seemed to play the role of the doting son, willing to go along with his parents' wishes. However, Stone did learn that Jack was a good enough quarterback that, with a little coaching, might amount to something. He also learned that the boy threw in the high eighties as a pitcher. None of this information could be verified; he got it by just talking to the school's athletic director Ted Morgand informally.

Evidently, once the story of their decision leaked, the Willow Brook people didn't take kindly to the Nortons looking to move out of their quiet, little community, let alone to a place like Hillsdale. They seemed to have been counting on Jack to give them a much-needed boost in both football and baseball this coming year. As a junior, he had been the only all-conference player in both sports, and the faithful really believed there was a chance for hope. The Nortons felt differently.

The original phone call to the State office came from an unidentified cell phone caller, claiming he was part of the Willow Brook district. Another followed shortly from the principal's office at Willow Brook High School. He lodged an official protest against Hillsdale High School, alleging that a member of the coaching staff of Hillsdale High School illegally contacted Jack Norton, trying to get him to come to Hillsdale. This was a violation of the state's recruiting laws.

When Stone had visited with the Willow Brook people yesterday, they had maintained that Ben Reynolds had shown the Nortons a football highlight video in a public restaurant. To them, that was an arrogant act of snobby "uppitiness." "Cheaters!" was the cry.

Stone had tried to decipher the basic information from the emotions. If the Willow Brook people were right, this was a major deal, as stupid as it appeared to be. However, until he learned the Hillsdale side of the story, he wasn't going to draw any conclusions.

Thomas just kept analyzing Jason's notes as the pair drove down the interstate. He continued to say nothing, so Stone had no idea what he was thinking. He thought about asking him if he had any questions, but he decided against it.

Instead, he began to focus on the questions he would pose to the Hillsdale people, especially Coach Ben Reynolds. Stone couldn't really believe that a person of Stone's reputation in the state would be so blatant to publicly recruit a player in a restaurant. "He's probably either just plain brainless or a bit naïve," he thought.

The car departed the highway at the Hillsdale exit in the same silence it had begun.

July 25

Chapter 12

Bubba Brown still may have owned his home in Hillsdale, but, to most people in town, he was nothing more than a Benedict Arnold. He and his family had very few friends remaining there, but with the situation they had created, there really wasn't much time for a social life. Whenever Helen went to the store for groceries, the clerk would be respectfully courteous, but nobody went out of their way to make her feel overly welcome. The Browns did most of their shopping at the Super Wal-Mart, where they could get easily lost in the size of the building. They rarely ate out, and if they did, they avoided the sit-down restaurants, settling mainly for the drive-thru of either McDonalds or Dairy Queen. For the most part, they tried to keep a low profile.

That's why it was rather surprising to see Bubba's beat-up Chevy pickup truck pulling into *The Cabin*'s parking lot. He hadn't eaten there since about a month before he had originally left for Valley Forge. Nobody paid much attention to him whenever he had come in before; normally he sat right at the lunch counter by himself. On this morning, he sported a three-day beard and looked to be on some sort of a mission.

Bubba walked through the door, and the bell above the door chimed, just like it did when any customer came in. Four regular coffee drinkers in a booth over in the corner took a quick glance when they heard the bell to check the identity of the walk-in and immediately went back to discussing corn prices, ignoring the visitor. A couple of bankers sitting at a table also refused to acknowledge Bubba's presence. He stood at the door for a second and then meandered to a booth by the window.

Rachel Sawyer shivered as she saw Brown take his seat in her waitress area. She had dated Brad for a short time last winter, and she never had felt comfortable whenever his dad came around. She always thought he was eyeing her. The last person she wanted to see that day was Bubba Brown, but she was determined to do her job. Nervously, she edged towards the booth.

"Would you like a menu, sir?"

"Nope. Give me the 'Rancher's Special.' Eggs scrambled and hash browns rather than American fries."

"What type of omelet would you like to go with that, sir?" She was biting her lip.

"Western. And don't act like you don't know me, Rachel," he snapped.

She turned and quickly walked into the kitchen with the order. She let the door brush against her back as it closed behind her. Tears dribbled down her cheek, and the cook Jeff Fairchild was quick to notice.

"What's wrong, Rache?"

"Brad Brown's dad. He's in there, and I have to wait on him." A pause. "He's a freak," she mumbled.

"What's that moron doing here?" He looked through the service door's window. "Listen. Don't worry," assured Jeff. "He's not stupid enough to try anything here."

"I just want him to leave." She proceeded to take a couple of deep breaths. Surprisingly, Rachel started to get her composure back.

She returned to the dining area and poured Bubba a cup of coffee without saying anything. She then returned behind the counter and tried to look busy.

"What's the matter, Rachel? You don't want to talk?" Bubba smirked. "Don't worry, I won't bite." That toothless grin shone again. "Oh, yeah, Brad said to tell you, 'Hi!'"

Rachel's back was to him, but he could see that last comment hit home again. Her shoulders sagged and then looked like they were shaking. Their wintertime split had not been a good one.

Brown then laced into the patrons inside the restaurant. "Well, here we are! The great town of Hillsdale! Boy, you guys ain't changed a bit, have you Buford? Have you, Elmer? Have you, Walter? Don't act like you don't know me! Or don't hear me, you phony bastards! You have to go to frickin' Willow Brook to get players! The great damn Hillsdale Hillmen have to go to tiny Willow Brook to get football players!" Bubba leaned back in his booth, stirring his coffee. He really didn't care that nobody in the place reacted to his harangue. The rest of the folks just kept doing what they were doing, as if nothing had even happened. A dense quiet permeated the dining area.

With no one to challenge him, Brown kept going. "You see! I was right! I was right all along! Cheaters! That's what you are! Nothin' but a bunch of damn cheaters! And the biggest cheater of all is that damn sonuvabitch Reynolds. He's the biggest asshole of you all! It's guys…!"

He never saw the plate. Suddenly, an omelet, hash browns, and scrambled eggs landed on his t-shirt and rolled down to his lap. "For Chrissakes! What the hell is going on? Who the hell…" His coffee cup spilled when he tried to catch the plate. The booth was a mess.

Jeff Fairchild stood above him with a menacing look. "Here's your breakfast, sir. Hope you enjoy it." His chest swelled.

Bubba jumped to his feet. "Why you…" The food spilled to the floor, and Brown almost slipped as he stood. He clenched his fist and struggled to gain his balance. Jeff was a rock, except that his eyes glared and his chest was heaving. The two stood nose to nose for a brief second. Once Brown noticed that Fairchild was about his size, he thought twice about it, looked around the room, and then stormed out the door. "Hillsdale sucks!" echoed from the parking lot.

Jeff bent down and began to clean up the mess. Rachel was quick to help. One by one, all of the patrons came over to lend a hand.

The beat up Chevy truck squealed its tires as it sped out of the parking lot.

Somewhere, Ray and Elise Johnson were smiling.

July 25

Chapter 13

Coach Ben Reynolds sat in the school board room by himself. He wore his usual golf attire, an Ashcroft polo to go along with his Dockers shorts. Like most Tuesdays, he was heading to the golf course to play his weekly match with Marty Pattin, a guy who worked out with him at the racquetball court during the winter months. During the summer, they would play 18 holes a week, wagering a dollar a hole. Ben had already earned $20 of Marty's money the past three weeks, so part of him was looking forward to the morning's fun in the sun.

However, the other part was really having difficulty understanding this State matter. Nothing about it made sense, other than it gave him just one more reason why he knew that getting out of coaching after this year was a great idea. Ever since he had been called in to discuss the situation with Alton Hubbard, the principal, the day after his birthday, he just couldn't figure out what all the fuss was about.

He told Hubbard everything, which really wasn't anything. This family called him, asked to meet him, and he met with them. The school knew beforehand, since this had happened before. He told Hubbard that he had advised the family to visit the school and talk to school officials, which they did the next day. He even told Hubbard about the DVD and the reason he showed it, since it wasn't a promotion or anything like that.

Jack Norton waited until the first of July to register at Hillsdale. The family was having trouble selling their house in Willow Brook, and they wanted to make sure all the round pegs fit into the round holes before they came to Hillsdale. No matter, the Nortons were coming; everybody seemed to know it. To Reynolds, though, this hadn't been the second coming of Peyton Manning or anything. The boy showed up the majority of the time at volunteer workouts, and he came to football camp, but again, to Reynolds, nothing would even matter until the first day of fall practice. That's when he would see whether Jack Norton could help the Hillmen or not; that's when he would see whether any single one of his twenty-one seniors would be the type of players he wanted on his team; whether the nineteen juniors were good enough to become varsity candidates; whether any of the thirty sophomores deserved a long look. Football practice has always been the way Hillsdale Hillmen were developed. The rest of this summer stuff was just show.

"Evidently, someone else cares. Who?" he thought. "With all the crap that goes on in this state, with all that the private schools pull in the suburbs each and every year, why has this become an issue? It's nothing."

A little exasperated, Ben stood up and faced the huge oval window that faced the faculty parking lot. An SUV pulled in to an empty stall.

July 25

Chapter 14

After thirty minutes of fruitless phone calling, Tim Hallion decided to quit. None of his usual contacts knew any more than he did. The only person he hadn't called was Mark Lowery, an old radio voice from Hillsdale. Lowery had been the "Voice of the Hillsdale Hillmen" for over twenty years at *99.9 WZJE*, but network executives had unceremoniously dumped him when a new group took over about three years ago. Hallion had heard that the new execs didn't like the fact that Lowery would spend nights in local saloons or bars after broadcasts. They felt that projected a negative image for their station. In those twenty years, though, Lowery had never been late for work, nor had he ever been late for a broadcast, and the people in Hillsdale loved his style.

Mark Lowery was a throwback announcer, the rah-rah guy who wore his heart on his sleeve each and every game, just the kind Tim Hallion felt high school kids still needed. He wasn't even a Hillsdale native; in fact, he migrated from Ohio back in the eighties, but once he took the airwaves, he left no doubt to that the listeners where his loyalties lay.

Hallion remembered when he was in high school at Northtown, listening to one of his broadcasts. The station would replay a tape of the game from Friday night on Saturday morning, a great idea, Hallion thought, something he wished Northtown had done when he was playing. Lowery's "Touchdown" call sounded like a bad stereo job of mixing the voices of ABC's Keith Jackson and the late Lindsey Nelson. That nasally "Touchdownnnnnn... Hillmennnnnn!" would echo through the crowd and, Hallion had learned through his web site, would also be a staple at all Hillsdale pep rallies from the student body. When Coach Reynolds finished his pep talk to the students, he always asked what they wanted to yell at the game that night. In unison, the student body would echo, "Touchdownnnnnn...Hillmennnnnn!" People worshipped him in Hillsdale, and they weren't too happy when he was let go. Some radio advertisers even pulled their sponsorship, but the company wouldn't change its mind.

Tim had lost track of Lowery in the last year or so. Earlier, Lowery had been an excellent source of information for "Rocco's Rocks," and the two of them had always gotten along very well. Supposedly, Lowery was still in the area, working for a country bar on the outskirts of Hillsdale. Hallion knew that if anybody could tell him anything about the Reynolds' situation, Mark Lowery would.

He quickly accessed his mailing list with phone numbers, addresses, and e-mails from contacts all over the state, and found Lowery's number. "I don't know if he will be up yet," Hallion muttered, "but, at least, I can leave a voice mail. He could be just coming in."

He punched up the numbers and waited. One ring, Two rings. Three rings. Four rings.

Finally, a sleepy voice picked up. "Hello."

"Mark Lowery? Hi, hope this isn't too early. This a voice from the past. Tim Hallion. From 'Rocco's Road.'" He hoped to jar Lowery into remembering.

"Yeah," yawned Lowery. "What the hell....who is this?"

"Tim Hallion. You know, 'Rocco's Road.'"

"OK, I got ya.' Tim, OK." He was starting to gather his senses, Hallion thought. "What the hell time is it?"

"Little after eight. Listen, I'll get right to the point and let you go back to sleep. I need some help and thought maybe you could give it to me."

Another yawn came over the phone line. "Me? How can I help you out?

"Listen, I need to know what you know about the Reynolds' situation. My web site is getting lots of hits suggesting he might be in some trouble. Nobody I've talked to can even give me any concrete information, other than it's supposed to be a recruiting problem with some kid from Willow Brook. Why in the Sam Hell would Ben Reynolds want a kid from Willow Brook? I've also heard that Bubba Brown might be behind the whole thing. Everybody knows what an asshole that guy is. I just thought that if anybody knew anything in Hillsdale, it would be you."

A pause of about four seconds was the initial response.

"You still there, Mark?"

Another pause. "Yeah. Listen, I'll tell you what I know. You're gonna keep this confidential, aren't ya?"

"Sure. Okay, I'm ready."

"I think Hillsdale is in a little trouble....."

July 25

Chapter 15

"Nice job, kid!"

"Way to be Jeff!"

"That was awesome, man!"

"You sure showed him!"

The congratulations came from all of the patrons. Buford, Elmer, Walter, everybody, even the bankers. They were not only glad Jeff stood up to Bubba Brown, but they were also a little pleasantly surprised Jeff Fairchild was the guy who did it. After all, Jeff Fairchild wasn't known for his heroics or any kind of temper.

The mess was quickly cleaned up just as the manager Bill Roberts walked in the door from an early bank run. He noticed the commotion. "What's going on?" he asked.

A chorus of voices responded in unison. "Jeff just kicked Bubba Brown's ass." "Jeff just ran Bubba Brown out of here." "Your man here is a hero."

Jeff stood rather sheepishly, not knowing how to respond to all of this sudden fame. "That guy's a jerk. He's always been one. He first was giving Rachel a hard time, and then he was bad-mouthing Hillsdale and Coach Reynolds and all. I guess I kinda lost it."

"What'd you do?" Roberts wanted to know.

"Uhhhh, I dumped his breakfast all over his lap," Jeff replied. "Don't worry, Mr. Roberts, I'll pay......" He was interrupted by another round of applause from the customers.

"No, you won't. I will." "Uh-uh. I've got it." "No way, it's on me." Money seemed to be flying all over the place.

"Wait, everybody. Nobody's paying. I'll just put it on Bubba Brown's bill," Roberts said, sarcastically. Everybody knew Bubba Brown didn't pay any bills, not while he lived in Hillsdale, anyway. "Okay, folks. The excitement's over." Jeff strolled back into the kitchen, rather embarrassed, while the others went back to their tables, still talking about what they had just witnessed.

The whole situation had happened so fast; he had merely reacted. First of all, Bubba Brown was a loudmouth; always has been and always will be. Second, the man's rude behavior affected a friend of his. Rachel Sawyer was a class act, and no way should a girl like her have to put up with an idiot like him. Finally, he committed the ultimate by slamming Hillsdale and Coach Reynolds. To Jeff, that was like Benedict Arnold dissing George Washington.

In truth, though, he just saw a situation that wasn't right and did something about it, just like he had been taught. That was something his dad had preached to him ever since he was a kid. He never planned to dump the food; it just seemed like the most obvious thing to do at the time. He also didn't know if he would have fought Bubba Brown, but he was ready to do what needed to be done. He was surprised at how fearless he had been; after all, Bubba Brown was both older and bigger.

However, once the excitement died down, Jeff Fairchild wanted no part of the spotlight. He never was one to seek attention. He did what he felt he had to do, and now it was over. He reached up and grabbed the next order to be met. As he grabbed a hold of the flour, he felt a hand on his shoulder. He turned around.

Rachel's smile overshadowed the tears that were now drying on her face. She leaned forward and kissed Jeff on his cheek. "I can't tell you enough how grateful I am for what you just did," she said softly. "Nobody has ever stood up for me before. Nobody. Especially against a guy like him. You were awesome, Jeff. I'll never forget it…or you." She clasped both of her hands around his waist for a brief moment and then turned and went back to work.

Jeff stood there, dumbfounded. He slowly reached up and rubbed his cheek where she had kissed him, knowing that he was blushing more than ever. Quickly, Jeff got back on task.

"Pancakes will be ready in a minute."

July 25

Chapter 16

Julie Reynolds was in a hurry. It was her turn to videotape a segment for an upcoming United Way promotional video they were going to use in a couple of weeks at their kickoff breakfast. All of the United Way board members were asked to tape the various agencies in the Hillsdale community in action, and Julie had volunteered to take care of the Salvation Army's "Back to School Giveaway."

Julie was not a morning person. Her husband had been long gone for his weekly golf outing. He had said something about stopping at the school first to talk to Alton Hubbard about those ridiculous rumors. So, she had lay in bed just a little bit longer than normal and had fallen back to sleep.

Luckily, Champ jumped on the bed and began to lick her face, or else she might still be sleeping. At any rate, she needed to be at the Salvation Army by 9:00, but she needed to pick up some new mini-DVDs at Wal-Mart first.

Julie really enjoyed her work for the United Way. It gave her a chance to see how many people in the community rallied around those sometimes less fortunate. She had a special spot in her heart for the Salvation Army, ever since she was a little girl and she first heard those bell ringers at Christmas time. Now, she took her turn each holiday season to be a bell ringer and had convinced everyone in her family to join in. It seemed, though, that whenever the Reynolds' turn came, it was always bitterly cold. But they always were one of the top volunteer families in collecting money.

She pulled out of her driveway and came to the four-way stop sign. She saw the clock on her car radio and knew that if she could get in and out of Wal-Mart in ten minutes, she would be on time. She put her turn signal on and began to ease into the road.

She never thought the pick up truck would run its stop sign.

July 25

Chapter 17

Bubba slammed on the brakes and tried to swerve out of the way. The tires screeched on the pavement, but Brown couldn't avoid the collision. He hit the sedan flush in the front panel on the driver's side.

The car spun as a woman's screams echoed down the street. After two complete twists, the vehicle came to a stop in the middle of the road. From his cab, Bubba could see the air bags of the car had gone off, and the horn was stuck.

Brown quickly got out of his truck and surveyed the situation. Amazingly, his truck didn't seem to be damaged at all, just a nasty dent in the front fender and some of the rusty paint scraped off. From the type of impact, he expected much worse. He ran up to the car and checked out the condition of the driver.

He was shocked to see that the driver of the car was Julie Reynolds, the coach's wife. She seemed to be groggy and incoherent, leaning on the steering wheel. Blood trickled along her forehead. Brown quickly looked from his left to his right. No cars. No trucks. Nothing. Nobody

It was already bad enough that the deal at *The Cabin* had happened. That Fairchild kid! He'd get him later. Now this! He couldn't get stuck with this, too. He raced back to his truck and shot down a gravel back road some hundred yards away towards Valley Forge.

"They would crucify me here if they found out I hit Reynolds' wife!" he reasoned.

Julie Reynolds' car just sat in the road, its horn still blaring.

July 25

Chapter 18

Ben Reynolds clicked the remote, turning the DVD player off. He pressed the eject button and removed the DVD and put it back in the case.

Fingers rolled on the legal pad, providing the only sounds in an otherwise very still conference room. "Thank you Coach Reynolds for being so detailed." That had really been the longest sentence out of Tom Thomas' mouth all morning. Jason Stone was writing furiously, trying to capture the answers given by Ben Reynolds the best he could. A tape recorder lay by, but none of the Hillsdale people were willing to use it. Not for this, anyway.

Ben Reynolds leaned back in his chair, sipping his third glass of water of the morning, but failing to satisfy his parched throat. Alton Hubbard sat stoically to his left, while recently named Athletic Director Jon Robbins nervously fidgeted in his chair to his right. Neither had been much help during this "series of questions." They had just sat there and let Ben handle everything. "Big time players aren't supposed to disappear in crunch time," Reynolds scowled under his breath.

Stone wanted to clarify what he had learned. "Okay, Coach. You say they called *you*, right?"

"That's right."

"You met them at …what's it called… *The Cabin*, right?"

"Yes."

"You never gave them anything, promised them anything, offered them anything? You didn't give them schedules or dates or anything like that?"

Reynolds was weary of all this. "Gentlemen, is this a trial? Am I getting accused of something illegal?"

"No, sir," Stone responded. "This is an inquiry. Allegations have been made, that's true, and our job in a case like this is to check out everything. So, did you?"

Reynolds responded firmly. "No. I gave them nothing. They may have taken a camp brochure from the store counter after I left; I don't know. Or they may have gotten one at the school the next day; I don't know. However, I gave them *nothing!*" He was starting to get irritated.

Stone was unperturbed. "Good. When they did move here earlier, they never asked you for help in finding a house?"

"Anybody who moves will go to either *Louis' Realty* or *Frank's Realtors* to find a house. It's not like Hillsdale is a Mecca or anything. If anybody were to ask any Hillsdale person about housing, they would send them to one of those two places. My wife works for *Louis'*. They chose the other guys. Don't make a big deal about something like that," he cautioned.

Thomas abruptly spoke up. "Coach Reynolds, it's out job to decide what's a "Big Deal" and what isn't. We'll make that call, Coach." He was not smiling.

Neither was Reynolds. Hubbard finally chimed in. "Gentlemen, I think this conversation has gone on long enough. We have cooperated fully with everything your department has asked us to do. Coach Reynolds volunteered to talk to you today. He really didn't have to be here. We really were under no obligation, but we want this mess cleared up as soon as possible. Hillsdale has always run a first class program, and I, for one, am a little insulted that we have been subjected to this line of behavior."

"Wow!" Ben thought. "I didn't know Hubbard had that in him."

Nervous Jon Robbins then spoke up. "Wwwwe haven't ddddone anything. We're innnnocent," he stuttered. Sometimes, Ben thought, people should know when to just stay quiet.

The two administrators began to rise, indicating the meeting was over. Jason Stone read their faces and realized that their morning's work was over. It was time to decipher the information with Tom Thomas and report back to Monty Phillips.

Ben Reynolds noticed that Thomas wasn't moving. "Is there anything else?"

Thomas responded," Uh, could we have a copy of that DVD to take with us? We might want to see it again."

"Why?" Reynolds asked. "You saw it. Nothing to it. You don't need one."

Hubbard overruled him. "Coach, we have nothing to hide. Go burn him a copy. Maybe it will finally bring this headache to an end."

Reluctantly, Ben Reynolds shrugged and left the room. Stone and Thomas began to gather their materials and got ready to head back. Stone said, "Thanks, Mr. Hubbard and Mr. Robbins. You really have done more than you needed to. We should be able to end this inquiry rather shortly. A few days at the most. We just have one more area to check out." That was a standard lie he had been taught to say, convincing the parties that there was still more work to do, whether there was or not.

"Let's hope so. We don't want Hillsdale's name dragged through the mud. We've done nothing wrong." Hubbard extended his hand.

"Bbbby the wwwway," interrupted Jon Robbins. "Dddoes a guy named Bbbbuba Bbbbrown have anything to ddddo with this?"

"Not that we know of. But again, we're not quite done," smiled Thomas, his eyes narrowing as he spoke.

Suddenly, the intercom rang out, "Coach Reynolds! Coach Reynolds! If you are in the building, report to the office immediately! It's an emergency! Coach, it's an emergency!"

July 25

Chapter 19

"Don't worry, Mark. I won't say a word. Thanks. Goodbye."

The man behind "Rocco's Rocks" hung up the phone very slowly. He rubbed his chin and scratched his elbow. If the information Mark Lowery had just given him was really true, Tim Hallion had a blockbuster piece of news.

Bubba Brown was setting up Hillsdale. First he called Willow Brook school officials and planted the seed. He then had called the State and accused Coach Ben Reynolds and the Hillsdale school district of illegally recruiting that Norton kid from Willow Brook. Brown had disguised his voice and used an alias, some name connected with Willow Brook, just to get the ball rolling. He meant to drag both Reynolds and the school through the mud to get back at them for the way they treated his son this past spring. Brown had given the State just enough information to make it look legitimate. Evidently, Brown had learned of the transfer and concocted the rest of the story. It must have worked since the word was out on the street in Hillsdale that a state official's car was seen in Willow Brook recently around the high school. Lowery's sources had been two beer distributors who lived in Willow Brook, guys who had stopped in his bar. Not the most reliable Hallion reasoned, but intriguing nonetheless.

Now what?

Run it, or not? Include Bubba Brown??? Can I prove that he's involved?

Check it out some more, or just print it as is?

Ignore it until somebody else brings it up online?

Run it as gospel?

These thoughts raced through Tim Hallion's mind. So much of him did not want to believe this information, yet the journalist in him said, "Go ahead!"

He grabbed his laptop and began to type, "Rocco's Blog......From Hillsdale, some troubling news that, if true, could mean a whole lot of trouble for the Hillmen football program and Coach Ben Reynolds....."

July 25

Chapter 20

Mark Lowery sleepily tried to hang up the phone. He missed the receiver on the first try but made it on the second. He leaned his head on his hand as he lay on his side.

"Some people will believe just about anything. Tim Hallion, well, you're not the first one, stupid; you just joined a long, long list of saps," he said to himself. "Bubba Brown probably doesn't even own a cell phone; two beer distributors from Willow Brook? How would I know that?" He chuckled and then rolled back over to the middle of the bed.

He didn't remember her name, but the night had been exciting. "Now, my dear, where were we before that rude interruption?" The giggling continued under the covers.

July 25

Chapter 21

Like most people around the country, fans have the perception that all football coaches are supposed to be tough, hard-nosed men who rarely let others see their emotions. Whether it's the NFL, Division I, or the local high school, the faithful seemed to admire those stalwart, square-jawed, committed leaders who are willing to internalize their feelings.

Ben Reynolds was never one of those. Oh, he was tough and firm all right, but he always had worn his feelings publicly. He loved giving high fives to his players when they made a great play; he even began using head butts—his head to the player's helmet---for extra special moments. He also added the "Doink" sound as well. His famous uppercut pump of the fist after a touchdown could only be matched by his high-step skip as he led his team out onto the field before each game.

His behavior at practice sometimes bordered on the eccentric. He often would quote lines from movies or break into a song when he felt the situation dictated. Once, after a young quarterback struggled to complete his throws during a passing drill, Coach Reynolds walked up, put his arm around the youngster, and said, "Son, that's not good enough for us to win. Can I tell you something? Can I tell you the truth?" Then, without batting an eye, he spun his hat sideways and broke into Jack Nicholson's Colonel Jessup from *A Few Good Men*, "You can't handle the truth! .....So get out there and perform like you can." He followed that with one of Nicholson's wry grins. Once the young man stopped laughing, he went out and performed admirably.

From the drawl of John Wayne to the falsetto of the Barry Gibb, from the special tones of Elvis to the undertones of Marlon Brando of *Godfather* fame, players never knew what might emerge from his brain. It certainly kept everybody loose, and Reynolds' motive was to maintain attention span for his squad. He explained to his coaches, "The average attention span of a high school player is less than a minute, so whenever I feel the guys need to be brought back on board, I'll do whatever comes to my mind."

The team would also see his "Dark Side" occasionally. He wasn't as bad as he used to be twenty years ago when he first began coaching, but if he ever got mad, his fuse was short. Jump offside or miss an assignment or not be aligned properly or not communicate with teammates—these were among the mental errors he just would not tolerate. He had struggled early in his career being overly sarcastic and sharply critical towards physical mistakes on the field, as well.

Once a defensive back named Bill Trainor had a clear shot at an interception right in front of the Hillmen's bench. If he had caught it, he probably would have run it back for a touchdown. Instead, he made the "Bingo!" call, as all Hillsdale DBs make when they are about to get a pick, but the ball went right through Trainor's hands, hit him in the chest, and bounced over his head, right into the waiting arms of the opponent's wide receiver who turned it into a touchdown for his team.

Reynolds went ballistic on the Hillsdale sideline, screaming everything under the sun at the dejected Trainor. The young man sauntered to the bench and turned to sit down with his coach hot on his heels. Reynolds was just about to deliver one last blast when the young man spun around and looked up at his pleadingly, "Coach, I didn't try to drop that pick. I didn't try to."

Reynolds immediately stopped in his tracks, swallowed deeply, and patted Bill Trainor on the helmet. "Son, you're right. You'll get another chance…real soon." Then it was the coach's turn to bite his lip and return to his duties.

And while the joy that followed victories was euphoric at times, the bitterness of the defeats, few though they were, agonized the Hillsdale mentor. If Hillsdale won, it was because the Hillmen players executed the game plan, and all the praise went to them. However, if the squad lost or, even worse by Coach Reynolds' standards, failed to play up to their capabilities, he would only blame himself for the results. He didn't have them prepared; he didn't cover this one phase enough; he didn't do a good enough job explaining what he wanted; he allowed his players to become complacent. This endless list often dragged Ben Reynolds into a long night without much sleep, asking himself over and over, "What else could I have done?" Saturday mornings became drudgery at times, but he always seemed to be satisfied with his one-night "penance service," as he called it, and he was able to bounce back into reality by Saturday afternoon.

What really distinguished Ben Reynolds from other football coaches was his tendency to cry at times. Not blubbery, mind you, but Coach Reynolds would have no qualms, for example, about choking on his words on Senior Night as he addressed the crowd describing his senior players. After the last whistle of the final regularly scheduled home game, the entire squad would gather at the fifty yard line, and Coach would speak to the crowd about the merits of the young Hillsdale Hillmen who were wearing that uniform on that field for the final time. No matter what the score or the weather, the stands normally remained full for this moving event each year.

He normally had a hard time at the annual Football Banquet, as well, trying to explain the bonds that existed among his athletes and the coaches. He especially had a soft spot for his managers. During the season and, especially at practices, he was very demanding of them. Yet, at the end of the year, he would hug each one bear-like in appreciation for what they had given to the program as he presented each with a lavish gift.

These periodic displays of emotion were well-known by his family members. So, it came as no surprise that tears rolled down the cheeks of the fifty year-old husband of Julie Reynolds as he parked his car in the Emergency Room parking lot and raced into the waiting room.

"Coach, follow me. Your wife is down the hall." Ben should have known the name of the ER nurse; she had been a student of his five or six years ago, but right now, names didn't matter.

"Right in here," she said. The door was already open, and Ben stood at the door with his fist in his mouth. Julie lay on the gurney, eyes closed, head wrapped, with wires and cables connected to all kinds of machines.

Tommy and JoEllen were already there, sitting alongside their mother's bed, tears streaming down their faces. When she saw her father, JoEllen rushed to him in a huge embrace. "Oh, Daddy," she sobbed uncontrollably.

Ben squeezed his daughter hard as his son rose and stood next to the pair.

"Is she okay?" Ben wanted to know.

"She has a concussion. That much we know. We just have to wait until the tests come back," the nurse replied. "She's resting comfortably right now, but we won't anything until the doctor reads the test results."

Ben nodded. The three Reynoldses stood in the middle of the room, arms around each other's waist. Ben whispered, "Let's pray, kids. Together.....Our Father, who art in heaven…"

July 25

Chapter 22

Bubba Brown rapidly wadded all of the bills he could grab out of Brad's top drawer and stuffed them in his pocket. He would repay his son later and maybe even offer an explanation. But now there was no time to waste. He counted the money he had in his wallet and figured he had enough to get the job done.

He hopped back in his truck and headed down the road, always looking for any sign of pursuit or police cars. Since he had left the scene back in Hillsdale, amazingly, he had encountered not one soul. Not one. He grinned at his good fortune. "So far, so good." He muttered.

It had been stupid for him to go back to Hillsdale that morning, but hindsight is always 20/20. At least he got out of there without being caught. He would deal later with that punk kid, what was his name???? He couldn't recall it off hand. ….And that Sawyer girl…he would see about her too.

He decided that he wouldn't tell Brad about his trip; no need to get him involved; Helen, too. She couldn't find out, because she would probably tell somebody. And if the cops question either one of them, what they don't know won't hurt them....or him, for that matter. No, only he needed to know.

He was proud of this new plan. Once he got this done, nobody would be able to trace his truck. He felt lucky... lucky that he got out of there without being seen. No way the Reynolds lady could have seen his face. No way.

Bubba pulled into *Valley Forge Auto Repair*. He got out of his truck and entered the front door. He yelled out, "Hey Joe, you here!"

A scraggly old man with suspenders entered the room. "Yeah, I'm here. Oh, Bubba, it's you. This morning's been kinda rough. We had way too many beers last night."

"Know what you mean. I told you I might bring my truck in. Listen, on my way home, I kinda banged into a tree in my front yard, so I was hopin' you'd knock out the dent in the bumper, Joe. I don't want to spend money on a new one."

"Lemme look at it," he replied, and then went outside to examine the damage. "Shoot, this is easy. Man, why don't you just paint this old thing? A new coat of paint to hide the rust and you might be able to get something for it if you wanted to trade down the line."

"You know, I've been thinking about that myself. How much would you charge?

"$300 for the whole job...Plus you have to buy the first round next time."

"All I got is $250. I don't get paid 'til Friday.

"That's okay. You'll need to leave it here for the next few days anyhow. You can pick it up Friday. We'll settle then…. over a few cold ones. Man, it's getting hot."

"Not as hot as it could be. Sounds good. Listen, I'll need something to get around in. You got anything?"

"Take that '99 Buick over there. It's like my spare vehicle, my loaner. You're not leaving town, are ya' in the next few days?"

"Nope. I think I'll sit in the AC for awhile. 'Til things cool down a bit. See you Friday, Joe." Bubba just couldn't wipe the smile off his face as he crawled into the vehicle.

July 25

Chapter 23

Tom Thomas was not happy. Not at all. They had been forced to leave Hillsdale without the DVD. When the call came over the intercom, all hell broke loose and the DVD didn't get copied. He had tried to get either Hubbard or Robbins to make him one, but they were far more concerned with Reynolds' predicament.

He slammed his folder on his lap. Jason Stone nearly jumped out his seat as he was driving. Just like the trip to Hillsdale, the return had been silent up to that point.

Stone saw his opening. "What's the matter?"

Thomas gritted his teeth. "We *needed* that DVD. Give us that and we got 'em."

"Got who?"

"Reynolds."

"Reynolds? How? That DVD wasn't anything. It was nothing but a bunch of pictures of kids and moms and a stupid song. That's all."

"You don't see, do you? That DVD was a highlight film. Showing that highlight film is a direct violation of the state mandate involving recruiting. Those Willow Brook people were right."

Jason almost swerved off the road. He couldn't keep from laughing. "Are you crazy? That wasn't any highlight tape. Highlight tapes show *highlights*, not kiddy photos. Nobody in his right mind would call that a highlight film. Nobody."

"Mr. Monty Phillips would. He's looking for something just like this."

"What about Bubba Brown? Are we checking him out at all?"

"What for? He didn't do any recruiting."

Stone couldn't believe his ears. "It's no good, Tom. Listen, you heard the stories from both schools. Sounds to me like Willow Brook is just crying cuz their boy decided to move. There's no recruiting here by Hillsdale. As a matter of fact, if anything, that Norton family recruited Hillsdale, not the other way around."

"You don't see, do you, Jason? Jason, Mr. Phillips has been the head of the State for only six months, and he has been looking a long time for a way to put his stamp on his tenure. He has made it very clear that he will not tolerate any signs of impropriety or cheating. He said that from Day One. If we were to find somebody, we are to nail them to the cross. I think he will judge that these Hillsdale people are guilty."

"Guilty? Guilty of what? Choosing poor music? Listen, if we want to nail somebody, then let's go after the Catholic

League. Or that guy in Valley Forge or the guy in New Frankfort.

Everybody knows that we could get something on those guys. Folks at the State have just been too afraid to take them on."

"Before you start passing judgment, keep in mind that you're one of US now."

"That's what I mean," Jason said. "Look, this is piddly-ass. Nothin' to it. But it has been great training for the bigger catch later." Their car passed over the river bridge. "Let's treat this like a fishing trip. This Hillsdale stuff; they're nothin' but the little fish. Let's throw them back and go after the big catfish."

"Jason," Thomas replied, "you're a dreamer. It doesn't matter the size of the fish. Any size of fish will do. We got our fish. And Monty Phillips will want us to reel him in."

Jason went silent. It would do no good to argue any more with Thomas. He would wait until he gave his report to Mr. Phillips himself. He would prove his point. Hillsdale was innocent. Reynolds was innocent. Jason would prove it to both Thomas and Phillips.

July 25

Chapter 24

Two hours later, Jason Stone picked up the phone and dialed.

"Good afternoon, Hillsdale High School, may I help you?."

"Hello. Mr. Hubbard, please."

"Mr. Hubbard is gone for lunch and then to the hospital to check on Coach Reynolds' wife. Would you like his voice mail?"

"Yes that will do."

Stone tried to choose his words carefully as he waited for the tone. He might as well be straightforward.

"Beeeeeppppp!"

"Mr. Hubbard, hello. This is Jason Stone from the State Athletic Association. Mr. Hubbard, Mr. Monty Phillips, the State Executive Director, requests that you make a copy of that DVD and get it to us as soon as possible. Preferably overnight mail. If you have any questions, you have my number. Thank you, Mr. Hubbard." Jason hung up the phone. His hands were shaking.

Part 3

August 9

Chapter 25

The afternoon session for the second day of football practice had just begun. The broiling sun and sweltering humidity made breathing difficult for the forty varsity members of the Hillsdale Hillmen, but they went about their business despite the discomfort with above normal enthusiasm. Their head coach had returned to practice that afternoon, his first activity in more than two weeks after his wife had been involved in a hit and run accident. He stood in the north end zone alone while his troops gathered together to begin their team stretch. Recovering from her injuries required a relatively long hospital stay for Julie Reynolds, as tests continued to come back negative, but the toll on her family had been even more taxing, especially for Ben.

Ben Reynolds had always taken pride in his ability to analyze and adapt to situations on the fly. The adjustments he had been forced to make as a coach during games over his career taught him to keep his focus and his feelings in check, which, for an emotional guy like he was, proved at times to be difficult. However, his reputation as a "game coach," one who seemed to be a step ahead of the opposition most of the time, was well-established in this part of the state. People marveled at how his play-calling would create a big play for his team or change momentum towards the Hillmen's sideline.

In his wife's case, though, Ben enjoyed no such luxury. For the first three days, Julie had remained unconscious, almost slipping into a coma on a couple of occasions. When she did come around somewhat, she was initially groggy, having a hard time recognizing any of her family members or friends. She seemed to slide in and out of "awareness," as Ben tried to put it. This lasted another two days. Ben felt helpless; nothing he could say or do could answer the myriad of questions that riddled his brain. Doctors and nurses weren't much help to the cause, either; they had no answers. So, he spent most of his time just sitting in Julie's room, holding her hand soothingly and petting her forehead while she slept.

Any time he was away from her side was spent in the chapel. Prayer had been something Ben had learned early in his childhood. "Ask and you shall receive," he remembered from his younger days. Several times he found himself on his knees in earnest pleading.

On the fifth night of the ordeal, Ben headed towards his nightly vigil in the chapel with his emotions sunk to their lowest point. The darkest thoughts normally come to a man when the unknown is involved, and Ben Reynolds had filled his mind with his utmost fears. Julie had shown no visible signs of improvement. He realized for the first time that he was afraid, afraid that Julie could become a vegetable or, even worse, possibly could die. He couldn't bear the idea of not having her around. He began to sob and lay prostrate on the floor, begging God to listen.

Then, on the morning of day six, with her husband at her side holding her hand, as was his practice, all of a sudden, Julie awoke, reacting as if nothing had happened. She just sat up in bed and wondered aloud where she was and how she got there. The miracle Ben had been praying for was finally answered. Just like trying to diagnose the original problem, the doctors had no logical or medical explanation for her recovery either. They just called it "an Act of God," something the Reynolds family wholeheartedly agreed with.

Two days later, after more tests revealed little of substance, Julie Reynolds came home. She was advised to lie in bed for a few more days, but the spunky Irish girl would have little of that. On her first day home, she decided to make biscuits and gravy for the whole family...for supper. Nevertheless, Ben had spent the past week waiting on her hand and foot to the point she finally had enough and ordered him back to football practice.

Julie could remember very little about the accident, other than it was an old pickup with rust spots. For Ben, that was okay. No sense reliving something we'd rather forget. But he decided he would like to get a piece of the person in the truck.

"Pffffhhht!" blew Head Coach Ben Reynolds whistle. "Position groups. Let's move." He began to jog towards his area. Two managers awaited him, each with a bag of footballs. He was ready to get back to work.

August 9

Chapter 26

She rinsed the pot rather slowly and methodically, just like she always had before, and then stacked it atop the other dishes she had washed by hand. Whenever given the chance, Julie Reynolds enjoyed doing dishes in the sink, rather than just filling and running the dishwasher. The radio crooned a Michael Buble hit in the background in almost a therapeutic style as she continued her task. She wiggled her fingers in the dishwater; she liked to joke to others that she believed the Palmolive liquid actually made her hands softer.

Julie shook the soap off her hands and wiped her hands on the towel draped over her shoulder. She turned around and inspected her kitchen. Spotless, just like always. "Spic and span," she smiled to herself.

These routine duties, to some, may have seemed boring and non-essential, but after what she had been through, Julie felt fortunate to be able to do anything. She normally enjoyed household chores; to her, having a clean house was as important to her as Ben's game plan each week was to him. Vacuuming, dusting, even washing floors were attacked with extra vigor each time she took the duty on.

Now that she was home from the hospital, she appreciated these tasks even more. "Let's face it," she told herself. "That was scary." And yet, she really didn't know why herself. The whole incident had been a blur, and she recalled nothing from the hospital stay, not until she finally woke up. She thought it was weird that after a couple of days, she floated in and out of consciousness because she had no recollection of any of it. In fact, she just thought she had been asleep for a week.

When she did wake up, she felt no pain, no soreness, nothing. However, she realized that things must have been very serious. One look at her husband's face told her that much. Once Ben stopped hugging and kissing her right in the hospital bed, he told her all that had been going on. Since she didn't remember any of it, she initially just laughed out loud as he told her the story. When she looked around the room, though, her two college kids, Tommy and JoEllen, were standing there crying, her husband was crying, even her mother who had traveled all the way from the southern part of the state was in the room crying, and all she could do was laugh. It was then she realized how lucky she had been.

The more tests the hospital ran, the fewer answers the doctors received. Julie spent most of her time in the hospital bed just trying to remember the details of the accident. The police came two, three times a day to question her in hopes that she might help somehow find this hit and run driver. She could see the stop sign, she knew she was going to Wal-Mart, and she could see the.......what was it???....It was a .....car..., no, a truck....a small pickup of some kind.... rust...That's all she could remember....for now.

Once released to go home, she felt she needed to get back on her feet as soon as possible, for two reasons. One, for herself----her competitive juices would not allow herself to stay in bed. Two, and more importantly, for Ben and the kids. Julie could see what a toll this experience had taken on the rest of her family, especially her husband. She needed to show everybody that she was okay.

Easier said than done, though. The kids and her mom were extra helpful around the house the first few days home, but Ben was almost ridiculous. She couldn't turn sideways without having him pick this up for her, bring her a drink of water, run the vacuum cleaner. He even tried to wash clothes; when he faded a pair of Tommy's jeans, though, that was it. She ordered him back to the football team. He finally went back earlier that afternoon.

After that, she sent the kids to the mall for Back-to-School shopping. The twins would be leaving for college in a couple of weeks, and they had lots to get ready. Julie felt that this second year of college would not be as emotional as their first one, so she didn't feel the need to go along with them this time. She then sent her mother to the grocery store to plan supper. She wanted some quiet time...alone.

The dishes done and the kitchen cleaned, Julie walked into the den where Champ was sleeping on the sofa. She parked in the lounge chair and put her feet up. With all the people around recently, she didn't have the chance to do what she really wanted to---picture the accident once again, all by herself.

Stop sign...sunlight...Wal-Mart....truck...pick-up.... As the images passed through her head, Julie felt there was one image that was just on the edge of her memory bank. Something or some face or some image was right there, and she felt the urge to see if she could focus.

She stared out the window....the stop sign...the truck, a small truck...about five feet away...what color was it?.... red?...rust?...anything special?...a dent?...a scratch?...a face?...a driver???...a bumper???...some decal???

Wait! Was there a decal?? What was it?? A blur....a design....something was there, but it wasn't ready to show itself...not yet..

Julie vowed not to stop until those images came clear. She got up and headed to the laundry room. Maybe next time.

August 9

Chapter 27

The past two weeks had been a living hell for Bubba Brown. He wasn't the mentally toughest creature around; he admitted as much. Keeping this low profile since the trip to Hillsdale had been much more difficult than he had thought. Whenever he went someplace, he avoided eye contact with most people, yet, at the same time, he felt that everybody was staring a hole right through him. He stayed away from one-on-one situations as much as possible; many of his meals for Brad and him were through the drive-up windows.

Like he figured, Brad had initially been angry when he discovered that his money had been taken. His dad assured him that it was a down payment for a better apartment for the two of them they were going to get later on, plus he would be paid back with 5% interest. That seemed to satisfy his son, but Bubba knew he would have to cover his tracks again later.

He was also glad he hadn't said anything to Helen. When she called later that evening and told him about Julie Reynolds being involved in a hit-and-run, he really played dumb and acted like he was honestly surprised by the news. "Not telling her was a good move," he thought. "If nobody knows, then nobody will find out." Bubba was proud of his logic.

He got his truck back in three days. Joe did a great job of straightening out the bumper and covering up the rust with a new coat of paint. He liked black better than red, anyhow. The truck had no signs of the accident on it at all. He really didn't know what he had to be afraid of. "It doesn't hurt to be cautious," he reasoned. So, he stayed in Valley Forge and did most of his driving in early morning or after dusk, just in case. He really didn't know "just in case" *what*, he just knew "just in case."

So, Bubba Brown's world had reduced to merely him and his truck. Brad ignored him even more than before, so he spent most of his time alone, with his thoughts and fears. But, when Joe called an hour ago and asked if he wanted to go out for a few drinks, he quickly jumped at the chance. And then when Joe offered to pick him up, that made him even happier. He could leave his truck under the carport.

He decided to shower and then shave. It was time to quit worrying and to start living a little again. He looked in the mirror in the bathroom. Wrinkles under his eyes and saggy cheeks---"Wow, I look like hell!"

He finished just as Joe's horn sounded out front. Bubba had a new bounce to his step as he skipped down the landing. Joe stood next to that same Buick Bubba had borrowed earlier.

"Hey, Bubba, let me see that tree you hit. You know, the night the last time we were out. Where is it?"

August 9

Chapter 28

"Chest over your knees, over your toes! Eyes in, head cocked. Good! Ready—One step, on me. Ready. Set, go! Set, go! Set, go! Set go!"

Coach Ben Reynolds continued to work his defensive backs through basic footwork drills, drills he had been doing for over twenty-five years. Drills he knew worked because they broke the game down so that a second grader could understand what was expected of him, if need be. Drills he knew could become second nature to any type of player at any level if practiced daily.

"Choppity-chop-chop! Choppity-chop-chop! Keep those feet moving! Eyes up! There's nothin' down there 'cept dirt! Good! Next group!"

If there was one place that Ben Reynolds felt at home, it was on the practice field. This was his classroom, and he roamed the grounds like a college professor explaining the latest theory. Every detail, every little step or angle, every position alignment, every reaction possible was treated with meticulous accuracy. The Hillsdale Hillmen had not reached the pinnacle of the

Midwestern Conference by being sloppy, and it was because of Reynolds' attention to detail that success was part of their legacy.

"Turn those hips! Stick that foot in the ground! Hold it! Hold it" he said. The group came to a complete halt. "Look, anybody can do these footfire drills...any body! If you want to be a solid high school defensive back, then you have to learn how to change directions! Now watch!"

He got into a proper defensive back stance and proceeded to teach them by showing them himself. He backpedaled a few feet, stuck his foot in the ground, and angled to the next cone in the progression. His form for a guy now fifty was a bit rough, but the players got the message.

"See, I can still do it" he said triumphantly, and then stumbled over a cone and landed right on his back side. The players laughed and quickly jumped back in to the routine. Coach Reynolds laughed at himself as well.

That's how Ben Reynolds had coached over his career, teaching, demonstrating, explaining, diagramming, and, occasionally, making fun of himself. Whatever it took to get his point across to his players, he was not be afraid to try.

The practice that afternoon focused on defensive principles. Ben normally called the offense during the seven-on-seven pass skeleton, letting Jerry Smith, his defensive coordinator, parade around his secondary and the linebackers. Smith, at times, got a little wild with the defense, but he insisted on having their motors running at full tilt all of the time.

"You'll never beat Valley covering like that! Get your eyes on the receivers, not the quarterback!" he yelled after the transfer quarterback Jack Norton completed the first three offensive plays. Even though this was just the second day of practice, the intensity was exactly what Ben Reynolds wanted. He could see that his assistants had established the players' focus during his short absence.

Finally, the defense began to squeeze the receivers a bit better, getting knockdowns on back-to-back plays. It was Coach Smith's turn to get excited. "That's it! Now you're getting' it! Great job!" he hooted. On play ten, Jeff Fairchild from his free safety spot read a crossing route and jumped in front of the receiver for an interception. Smith threw his hat into air, "Bingo! Bingo! Touchdown! Touchdown!" He raced alongside the startled Fairchild and kept running on by him, just as if he had picked it off himself and was on his way to the end zone.

Even though Norton's head was down with the result of that last play, Ben thought this was a good way to end practice. He blew his whistle and called his players together. They knelt down on one knee, removed their helmets, and listened to their head coach for the first time that season.

"Men, first of all, let me thank all of you, players, coaches, and managers, for all of the cards, the well-wishes, and the prayers over the past two weeks or so. My family and I, especially my wife Julie, are eternally grateful. You really helped us get through a tough time. She actually kicked me out of the house today and sent me here to practice, so I know she's feeling better." The players chuckled.

"Our coaches and you have done a great job these first two days. We have been successful at Hillsdale because both players and coaches care. They care about this program and they care about each other. That's what makes us special." The players nodded their agreement.

"That being said, we have sooooo much work to do before we play Valley Forge. Every practice, we have to take one step or two steps forward, never a step back. If each and every one of us makes every drill, every rep, every team situation count, we'll be ready for the Warriors. Remember, they're coming here this year, and we don't lose at home!" His eyes narrowed.

"Last of all, I don't know about you, but we've had enough excitement around here for awhile, what with Jeff and his deal and the accident involving my wife. There are people out there who just wait for us to stub our toes and make a mistake, a mistake that could drag our team down. No matter what, don't let that happen Let's be on guard. Okay? We are better than that."

"Tomorrow's the last day without pads. Be in the weight room by 6:30 in the morning ready to go. And study those playbooks! OK, everybody in here!" Players and coaches rose, came together, and raised helmets or fists in the air. "Hillmen on three….One, two, three. Hillmen!"

The noise echoed through to the school parking lot where a single figure stood alone, watching the proceedings intently.

August 9

Chapter 29

It took a lot of courage for Tim Hallion to get in his car and drive to Hillsdale that afternoon. However, he had grown sick and tired of the bashing Ben Reynolds and the Hillsdale Hillmen were receiving on his website. People who posted were, for the most part, simply ignorant of the facts that surrounded the situation, yet they felt compelled to lambaste the coach and the community. Calling for the coach's immediate firing, having Hillsdale forfeit every game since Reynolds took over, wanting them not to play the upcoming season at all as punishment, and putting Coach Reynolds' house on the real estate market were just a few of the more outlandish ideas he had screened.

The whole problem here, at least how Hallion saw it, was this major reaction was entirely his fault. Had he not written that blog about Bubba Brown, probably things would not have gotten as ugly as they had. People in Valley Forge who subscribed to his service had become virtually "hateful" towards those in Hillsdale. Those in Willow Brook were equally as bad. The Hillsdale faithful had just starting canceling their subscriptions. That hurt Hallion in the pocketbook.

Worse than that, though, was that Tim Hallion felt he had betrayed the people of Hillsdale and lost the confidence and support of a man he truly respected, Coach Ben Reynolds. Phone calls to the Reynolds's residence went unanswered, despite the numerous voice messages left by the young Hallion. He even tried the school, but the secretaries there told him that Coach Reynolds hadn't been in the building for the past two weeks. With the football season beginning, Hallion couldn't see the feasibility of that happening. He just felt they were giving him the run-around.

So he decided to drive to Hillsdale that day and confront Coach Reynolds face to face. He was intent on making things right; that he meant no harm to either him or the people of Hillsdale. He wanted to straighten out any misunderstanding he may have caused.

From where he stood in the parking lot, he could see the entire Hillsdale practice area. "No wonder," he thought, "these guys are always so good. Everything out there goes like clockwork. Precision, precision, precision. Repetition, repetition, repetition. Discipline, discipline, discipline. Up and down the line, that's what they do."

He saw the team meeting at the end of the workout and thought that would be as good a time as any to speak to Coach Reynolds. He swallowed, but nothing went down. He slowly walked towards the coach as he spoke to one of his assistant coaches. Coach Reynolds did not see Tim Hallion approaching, but Assistant Coach Jerry Smith did.

"What the hell do you want?" Smith snapped. "We don't need your kind here."

"I would like to speak to Coach Reynolds if I could," Hallion stammered. A pause. "Coach?"

Reynolds looked at Smith and then back at Hallion. With all the excitement in his life the past couple of weeks, he really didn't know either why Hallion was there or why Smith barked at him. He had been so wrapped up in taking care of Julie he had no idea of all of the commotion that had risen lately. Smith did.

"Coach, this is the asshole who ran that blog about Bubba Brown turning us in for recruiting. He can't be up to anything good," Smith's voice quivered.

"That's not entirely true. Listen, that's why I'm here. I want to set the record straight, Coach," Hallion addressed Reynolds.

"Just a minute. What's this all about? Smitty? C'mon, tell me." Reynolds said.

"That sonuvabitch" pointing directly at Hallion, "ran a story on his web site stating that Bubba Brown contacted the state about the Norton kid. Said we recruited him and the state is gonna come down hard on us ...and you! Everybody...in Valley ...Willow Brook... even here in Hillsdale are all honked off about it. Didn't you know?"

"No," Reynolds responded firmly. "I've been kinda tied up lately. I hadn't heard anything about this. Is this true, Mr. Hallion?"

Hallion took a deep breath. Sweat trickled down the back of his neck, and it wasn't because of the heat. Looking at Coach

Reynolds right in the eye at this juncture was one of the hardest things he had ever done. He searched for the right words.

"Coach, it's not what you think." He knew that wasn't a good way to begin, but he had to say something.

"What is it, then?"

"When I got word about a possible problem you guys were having, I didn't think there was any truth to it. Why would you guys want a kid from a town that hadn't won in over twenty years? It just didn't make sense. But all the people on my web site kept giving innuendos and hints that Bubba Brown was behind it all. I knew about last spring, so I decided I needed to check it out."

"Who'd you talk to?"

"That was the weird thing. I tried over twenty calls. Nobody knew anything."

"Did you think to call our school?"

"Not until the last day or so. But I was trying to have them help me find you."

"Did you try to call me about this?"

"Same deal. Not before I ran the story."

"How about Bubba Brown?"

"Never thought he would talk. Besides, not many even claim knowing where he is."

"So, where you'd you get your info?"

"Mark Lowery."

"*Lowery?* You gotta be kidding me. That butthole?" Coach Smith chimed in.

"Yeah," Tim responded, a bit bewildered. "I thought if anybody knew the truth in Hillsdale, it would be Lowery."

"Mr. Hallion," Ben Reynolds said dryly, "with all due respect, Mark Lowery would be one of the last people in Hillsdale I would trust. Ever since he got fired at the radio station last year, he's had a burr up his hind end. I think he blamed us for all of his problems, like we had something to do with his getting dumped. No. I don't think any of us would call Lowery "Hillsdale's finest.""

Coach Smith wanted to know, "What did he tell you?"

"He told me Bubba Brown was the instigator. He wanted to get even with Coach and Hillsdale about that deal with his son. It made sense at the time," Hallion replied. "So I ran with it. I thought I was printing the facts. I didn't know, Coach, I didn't know. I am so sorry. I feel like an idiot."

"You sh-" began Smith.

"Hold it!" Ben interrupted. "Mr. Hallion, what's done is done. We can do nothing about the past. You live in the past; you die in the past. We have to look ahead. With all that has happened with my wife, I haven't really dwelt much on this crap lately."

"I'm sorry, Coach. What happened?" asked Tim.

"A couple of weeks ago, she was involved in a hit and run. Pretty scary for awhile. I haven't had much time for anything else lately."

"Oh, I didn't know. I should have known, but I didn't. All these things I should have done first, but I didn't. I'm supposed to know things like that. I guess I'm not a very good media guy after all."

"You got that- " started Coach Smith.

Ben stopped him again. "Jerry!" he snapped. Then, in a calmer voice, he added, "At least now, Mr. Hallion has more of an understanding of our situation. I wish you had contacted us from the beginning. Nobody has heard our side, except for those state guys. We still haven't heard from them yet. Hopefully, nothing's gonna come from all this nonsense."

"Then," Hallion asked, "none of that stuff at all was true?"

"The Norton kid is here. He's been here. He's an okay player, nothing great. He may play some. Too early to tell. If anything, his parents came after us; we never went after him. We've heard about Willow Brook, too, ya' know." For the first time, a slight smile came to Ben's lips.

"Coach, I promise you this. As soon as I get back, I will print a retraction of this whole me…"

"Mr. Hallion, we still have a problem. Somebody did turn us in. If you want to help, find that guy."

"It's a deal. Ah, Coach?"

"Yeah?"

"Call me Tim, okay?"

"You just find that guy, or you will be called all kinds of names. Most of them, you won't want to hear."

With that, Ben Reynolds and Jerry Smith turned and headed towards the Hillmen locker room. Tim Hallion was left standing alone in the middle of the practice field.

August 9

Chapter 30

"Oh, that tree!" Bubba responded. "It's not around here really. That happened somewhere between here and the bar. I don't really remember exactly. I was, uh, pretty drunk, ya' know."

"Yeah, sure, I'll bet you never hit no tree. I'll bet you hit another car or something," Joe laughed. "You just don't want nobody to know. C'mon. Git in." He slapped Bubba playfully on the shoulder.

Bubba shuddered, but Joe didn't notice. Joe walked around to the driver's side, while Bubba quickly slipped in on the right. He thought it would be better to play along. "Yeah, Ol' Hit and Run Bubba; that's me." He managed a laugh, but it seemed a bit hollow. "Where we goin'?" he asked trying to change the subject.

"How about *Barney's*? They play that good old country there. Plus, tonight's 'Two for One,' and it's "Wings Wednesday," both regular and buffalo. You like wings?"

"Oh, sure." He really didn't like buffalo wings because they gave him heartburn, but Bubba was just glad the subject was changed. "You like hot sauce, Joe?"

"The hotter the better." Bubba noticed a strange odor in the car, like someone hadn't showered in awhile. He knew it wasn't him.

They drove along a few blocks with Joe echoing the praises of *Barney's,* when he wasn't just singing off key to whatever that station he was listening to. Bubba just let him go, peering out the window at the scenery. They had to pass Valley Forge High School on the way. Bubba suddenly had an idea.

"Hey, Joe. Mind if we pull over a minute here at the high school? Football practice is going on, and I kinda like to watch it to see how my boy is doing. It won't take long."

"Okay," Joe responded, looking at his watch. "Happy Hour doesn't start for another twenty minutes or so, so we can stay about ten to fifteen if you'd like."

"Thanks. Just pull into the parking lot over here." Bubba pointed to that familiar spot he had parked his truck those many times before. He hadn't had the courage to come to practice by himself in his truck ever since the trip to Hillsdale, despite its new paint color..

The Buick pulled in, and the two of them both got out. Joe said, "So, this is high school football, huh?" Out on the field the Warriors of Valley Forge were running through some offensive plays. All of a sudden, a whistle blew, and a coach's angry voice rose above the other chatter from the field, which then became eerily silent. The two men couldn't really tell what was being said, but, by the tone in his voice, that coach was not happy.

Bubba said, "Let's get a little closer. I love it when Coach Buchanan loses it on a kid. That's why Valley Forge will beat Hillsdale in a couple of weeks. That man knows how to coach."

Joe and Bubba edged their to the end of the parking lot where they had a much clearer view. Sure enough, Coach Buchanan was all over an unfortunate young man. "You go the wrong way again, you sonuvabitch, you'll never see this field. You got that!" Buchanan screamed. He then grabbed the young man's face mask, wrenching the head of the player in the process. "Do you hear me?"

"Yessir," came a muffled reply.

Bubba suddenly turned to Joe and blurted, "C'mon. Let's go. Now!" He hurried back to the car and got in. Joe followed shortly, a bit confused. "What's the matter, Bubba?"

"Nothing. I'd just seen enough. That's all." The car slowly turned and left the parking lot, heading to Happy Hour.

Back on the field, Brad Brown tried to straighten his face mask and adjust his chin strap as he got back to the huddle. He didn't want anyone to see the tear rolling down his cheek. "I hate my dad," he muttered to himself.

August 9

Chapter 31

He really didn't know why he decided to drive to Hillsdale again that afternoon, but Jason Stone felt the only way he could be satisfied with all the things that were bothering him about the Reynolds case was to keep digging.

These past two weeks had been exceptionally frustrating for Stone. Once Monty Phillips and Tom Thomas got their hands on that DVD from Hillsdale, they basically kept Jason in the dark about what the future lay regarding the case. Each of the daily briefings covered non-essential material or else information that would add nothing to the decision. Whenever Jason would ask about the DVD or Bubba Brown's role in the matter, the response was always the same, "When we think you need to know more, Jason, we'll tell you." Obviously, he was being shoved into the background.

Yet, he still wasn't satisfied. All of the logical points, he felt, produced no incriminating evidence against Hillsdale. So, if he was going to be a worthwhile investigator for the state, he decided he needed to search for information on his own.

As he left the highway, he noticed the old sign for *The Cabin*, a place that might give him some answers. Restaurants like this reminded him of home, of the times he worked at *Johnny's*, a neer-do-well stop in the road that served great food and provided him with great tips during his high school days.

He pulled into the parking lot of *The Cabin* just as another blue convertible was turning in from the other lane. He let the fancy-looking car go in front of him, and they parked side-by side. As the driver of the convertible got out, Jason told him, "Nice car."

A rather subdued Tim Hallion nodded, "Thanks."

The two walked into the restaurant together, but neither spoke. They each sat down at the counter, two stools apart. Hallion seemed lost in his own thoughts, while Stone studied the ambience of the diner. He especially noticed the picture of an elderly couple hanging above the cash register, the original owners he assumed. Around the walls hung photos of several athletic teams from Hillsdale High School, some of them going back thirty to forty years.

On one wall to his left, the more recent squads were set. A closer look told Stone that the majority of them included football teams from the Ben Reynolds' regime. Each team picture had the squad members' names listed underneath, along with a detailed summary of that unit's success during the season. What stood out, though, was the signature scribbled in the lower left corner of each. "Best Wishes to the Cabin Crew. Coach Ben Reynolds."

A smiling young lady came up to take their orders. "Today's special is Cabinburger and fries for $6. Have you made up your mind, sir?"

Jason smiled back. "Sounds good. Cook it medium well. Add a diet to that as well."

Rachel Sawyer then strolled down to Tim Hallion. "How about you, sir?"

Hallion had been oblivious to everything since he had sat down. He was still trying to figure out how to get to the bottom of this mess he had created.

"Sir? Can I get you something?"

"Oh, sorry. Sorry. I was thinking about something else. What's the special today?"

"Cabinburger and fries for $6."

"Yeah," he paused, glancing through a menu. "I guess that's okay. Give me a large root beer to go with that." He closed the menu and placed it back in its holder. He reached into his back pocket for his notebook, opened it and set it on the counter. He then pulled his pen from his shirt collar and drew a triangle on the pad. On the first point, he wrote "Bubba;" on the second he scrawled "Lowery;" and on the third he scribbled "Coach." Then he drew a line from "Coach" and wrote "State." He put his pen down and rolled his fingers on the counter top.

Rachel brought the drinks for both men. "A diet…and a root beer." She couldn't help but notice the notes on the pad. "Looks like you're an artist," she smiled.

"Not hardly," Hallion replied. "Just working on something."

"Oh, yeah. What?" she inquired.

"This crap about Coach Reynolds. Trying to get to the bottom of it."

Stone's ears perked up, but he chose to stay silent.

"Yeah," Rachel said. "You're not from around here, are you? Well, everybody around doesn't really think anything's gonna come of that. Coach is a good guy. He didn't do anything."

"Somebody did, though. You live here?"

"I'm a senior at Hillsdale."

"You know Mark Lowery?"

She frowned. "I don't know him personally. But I've heard of him. He used to be the radio guy 'til a couple of years ago. He's kinda gone downhill from there, from what people say.

"People? Who?"

"Customers in here are always talking. I've picked lots of stuff about people since I've worked here."

"What have you heard about Bubba Brown? He used to live here, didn't he?"

With that, Rachel flinched and quickly turned away. "I've got to get your order," she said, and hurriedly went back into the kitchen.

"She knows something," Hallion muttered to himself, sipping his root beer.

"Now's as good a time as ever to speak up," Jason Stone thought to himself. "I'm looking for Bubba Brown, too," he said, extending his hand. "Hi. I'm Jason Stone. I'm with the State Athletic Association."

Hallion was a bit startled at this revelation, so he hesitated. Stone's hand remained extended, and then Tim slowly reached out and grasped it. "Hi. I'm Tim Hallion." They shook hands, a little hesitantly at first, but then more assuredly.

Stone asked, "Don't I know you. I think I've heard of you before."

"Probably not me, but my alias. I'm Rocco, from *Rocco's Rocks*. You know, the web site. I run it."

"Yeah, you wrote that blog about Hillsdale and Bubba Brown, didn't you?"

"That's why I came to town today. Too much crap has come up about it. I gotta figure out a way to fix it."

"What do you mean?"

"I thought I had a reliable source regarding the reasons Coach Reynolds is in trouble with the State. Turns out that I was wrong, and I never should have printed that blog."

Rachel returned with their orders without any mention of the prior conversations. Here you go. Ketchup, mustard, and relish are all right here. Need anything else?"

"I'm good," Stone said.

Hallion responded, "Got any honey mustard?"

"Sure." She reached under the counter and set a huge jar in front of the media man.

"Thanks," he said, as Rachel turned to wait on a couple who had just sat down in a booth.

Stone took a huge bite from his burger. "Now," he said with a mouthful, "tell me about Bubba Brown and what you know about him."

Hallion began with some of the vile hits on his web site that began the furor and traced the story all the way to his conversation with Mark Lowery and his trip here that day to Hillsdale. With each bite, Stone picked up little tidbits of information that had been overlooked in his original investigation. As the details became more prevalent, Jason was convinced that his theory about Hillsdale and Coach Reynolds was valid, but checking out Bubba Brown more could only alleviate matters.

Stone returned the favor to Hallion by telling him all that he could about things he knew. Because of his role with the State, he couldn't say anything about the DVD, but he felt he at least owed "Rocco" some pieces of information.

Finally, the two finished their meal. "What now, Mr. Stone?" Tim wanted to know.

"Call me Jason. I guess we still need to know if all of these false accusations were started by Bubba Brown."

Rachel had just returned with fresh drinks but virtually stopped in her tracks as Bubba's name was mentioned again.

Hallion noticed. "Miss, that's the second time Bubba Brown's name has affected you since I sat down here. Something happen 'tween you and him?"

Rachel looked at both men, started to speak, but held back.

Jason tried to soothe her. "No need to worry. We are just looking for some answers. That's all."

She whispered, "I don't even know who you two are."

"Sure," Jason said. "I'm Jason Stone. I work for the State Athletic Association. I've been in charge of finding out the truth in this matter." He extended his hand again, smiling.

"And I'm Tim Hallion. You may have heard of my web site *Rocco's Rocks*. I'm Rocco." Hallion stuck his hand out as well.

Rachel smiled at Tim and shook his hand. "You, I've heard of. The boys talk about your web site all the time. Jeff Fairchild- he's on the football team and he works here—he checks on the site almost every day. They're still mad about that story you wrote about Coach."

"They have a right to be. That's why I'm here today. Found out I got some bad info. Tell them to read tomorrow's blog."

She then turned to Stone and shook his hand. "I'm Rachel. Rachel Sawyer. When the Browns lived here, I dated Brad for awhile. His dad was a total jerk then, and I found out recently he's still one. I can't stand him."

"What happened?" Tim asked.

"A couple of weeks ago, he came in here, to *The Cabin*, just a little after the story broke on Coach. He moved to Valley Forge last spring, but he still has a house here in town. He just never seems to be around much. So we were all surprised when he popped in." She pointed to a nearby booth. He plopped in that booth over there and started shootin' his mouth off to everybody in here. Talkin' trash about Hillsdale and Coach."

"What did he do to you?" Jason wanted to know.

"I had to wait on him. I didn't want to, cuz I knew he'd do something or say something. See, I dated his son once. But I had to; it's my job." She paused, her drifting back to that bitter memory.

"Then what?" It was Hallion's turn.

"He started dissing me, and then he really got nasty, yelling at everybody here in the restaurant. Cussin' and swearin' a blue streak. Just rippin' on Hillsdale and Coach Reynolds. It was awful."

Hallion again. "What stopped him?"

Rachel smiled. "Jeff...you know, that boy I told you about...he came out and dumped his entire order on his lap. Mr. Brown got up like he was gonna do something, but Jeff stared him down. Then he just took off in his red pick-up truck and squealed his tires out of the lot and headed down the road. That way" She pointed towards the south. "Down towards Wal-Mart."

"When did you say that happened?" Stone asked.

"Couple of weeks ago. The same day Mrs. Reynolds got in that hit-and-run. You heard about that?"

"Yeah," Hallion said. "Just did today." He got up suddenly from the counter, but Jason Stone had already beaten him to the door. The two raced out into the parking lot and peered down the road Rachel had just mentioned. "You thinkin' what I'm thinking?" he asked Stone.

Stone nodded. "Yep."

Rachel wasn't too far behind. "Hey you two, what gives? You didn't pay yet."

"Rachel, my dear," said Stone, "you just earned yourself one heckuva tip."

Both of the men chuckled as the trio headed back into the diner.

August 9

Chapter 32

Julie Reynolds decided to take a bubble bath, something she hadn't done for who knows how long. She felt she had earned it, with as much cleaning as she had done. Her kids were out messing around with friends; her mom was downstairs reading her book; and her husband was, where else, in the den watching game film on Valley Forge. "Well, at least he's back into some kind of football routine," she thought.

She added a little extra *Body Shop Bubbles*, along with some bright red aromatic liquid from *Bath and Body Works* her daughter had given her. She set the bottle down and waited for the tub to fill. She stood in front of the mirror, brushing her hair slowly. This had been the first time since she had come home from the hospital that she had actually spent time alone in the bathroom. She was still amazed that she had no visible signs from the accident, no scars, no bruises.

She tested the water and slid in, slowly sinking underneath the bubbles. She lay there motionless for almost a minute with her eyes closed, then splashed a little water on her face. She rose up and her eyes settled on the red bottle of bubble bath.

It hit her. The truck…. It was red, and rusty red at that. She could see it briefly, but she was sure she was right. The truck was red. With rust on the bottom. She knew it!

She slid all the way under the water and popped back up, covered with suds all over her face.

"Ben! Ben! Come up here, please! I got something to tell you! It's about the wreck!" she yelled, with a bubbly smile on her face. She could hear the footsteps racing up the stairs.

August 9

Chapter 33

Six hours after he had left to go for a few beers, Bubba Brown was dropped off in front of his apartment building by Joe. He stood on the sidewalk, searching for his keys in his pockets as the car drove away. After a bit, he stumbled towards the door and fumbled the key into the lock. He almost tripped coming in and he tossed his keys towards the table in the kitchen, but missed madly as they rattled onto the floor.

He turned on a light and sat in a chair and tried to take off his shoes. He looked towards his feet and four blurry feet appeared. He tried shaking the shoes off, and finally they came off.

He got up and went to the refrigerator to get a beer. No matter he had downed more than a dozen earlier that night. He needed a nightcap. He popped the top and sat back down again, guzzling the bottle. After a long swallow, the scene he had witnessed that afternoon at football practice returned. The thought that his son was singled out by Buchanan had unnerved him at first. He couldn't stand to see it happening.

But as he took the next drink, his mood changed. He began to get angry, angry at the coach. Not Buchanan, though. His thoughts turned back to Reynolds. He was the asshole who had made his family move in the first place. That idiot had caused so much grief to him, his wife, and his son. He would pay some day; he would pay.

Then his thoughts turned to Brad. How dare he get into trouble at football practice! How dare he blow everything they were working for! How dare he screw up his scholarship! How dare he embarrass the good Brown name.

He struggled to his feet and yelled to his son, "Brad! Brad! Wake up, you idiot! You screwed up tonight at football, and now you are going to answer to me!" He had trouble keeping his balance, but he found his way into the area where Brad lay sleeping, exhausted from a rough day at practice.

His son wouldn't answer, so Bubba shook the bed. Still no response. He pushed his son's shoulder. "Get up, you sonuvabitch! You're gonna answer for today!"

Brad rolled over, gathered his senses, and appraised the situation. He got up and stood facing his dad.

Bubba stepped towards him. "Brad, I'll te---" Bubba hit the floor hard, out like a light.

Brad rubbed his knuckles and looked at his father on the floor. One punch was all it took. He crawled back into bed and fell into a deep, satisfying sleep.

August 9

Chapter 34

......August 9....11:00 p.m.   This blog is long overdue. I have tried to develop a web site that you high school football fans can rely on for its honesty, its integrity, and its accuracy. I have spent many hours checking and analyzing information as I receive it before I let it appear on my site.

I didn't do that with the Hillsdale Hillmen/Coach Ben Reynolds situation. The information I used when I printed that initial blog came from a source I thought had been reliable, a source I trusted, a source who, I found out, misled me.

Based on what I have learned, I can tell all of my readers that we have no proof that the allegations slanted towards the Hillsdale community stated in the blog of late July are true, we have no proof that Bubba Brown was the instigator regarding Coach Ben Reynolds, and we have no proof that any violations from the State even exist. We do know that the State has investigated some claims regarding Hillsdale and Jack Norton, but nothing has come of those yet.

I apologize to any and all who have been offended, especially the people of Hillsdale and, even more so, Coach Ben Reynolds himself and his family. I cannot undo the damage this web site has caused, but I will ensure that I will do everything in my power to be 100% accurate before any more information is released by this reporter.

I am truly sorry. Thanks for reading.

Rocco

Tim Hallion posted his work, turned off the computer, and went to bed, feeling a little bit better about everything. He knew the next few days, though, were going to be interesting….quite interesting.

Part 4

August 20

Chapter 35

The starting lineups were pretty much set, and Jeff Fairchild's name was not among them. Despite his best efforts in practice, little mistakes along the way, like what happened in the previous night's scrimmage, caused him to be moved down to "back-up." He was a back-up defensive back, as well as a back-up wide receiver. The thought of his being labeled as a "reserve" was tough to take, now that he was a senior. He knew that nobody on the team knew the offense or the defense better than he did. Nobody had as much desire as he had, but the results that he wanted just hadn't materialized. He was "second team."

During the scrimmage last night, the final one before the start of the regular season, the one called "The Soap Game" for the past twenty-five years because everybody brought a bar of soap or a bottle of shampoo for the players in the locker room as admission, the big one in front of all of the fans who were getting their first look at the Hillmen for the upcoming season, he had stunk. He dropped three passes on offense, one of which came after a great move to get open and would have probably resulted in a touchdown if he had just caught the ball. On defense, it wasn't much better. Two times he slipped trying to guard Jake Lewis in man-to-man coverage, and both times it was six points for the White team. The only thing he did accomplish was make a couple of tackles on kickoff coverage, but nobody really pays much attention to stuff like that.

He was so disappointed that he didn't even bother to go to the dance in the cafeteria afterwards, even though Rachel Sawyer said she was going. Instead, he went to the cemetery to visit his dad's grave. He asked aloud if he was any good. He wondered aloud if he had just tried too hard. He questioned whether things would work out for him like he dreamed. During times like this, Jeff tried to rely on his dad's memory and inspiration to boost his spirits. He stayed there till after midnight with little solace.

Jeff took one last look at the depth charts posted in the locker room, and then began the short walk to the coach's office. On top of this one disappointment, now Coach Reynolds wanted to talk to him. Getting called into the coach's office by himself after practice that morning was definitely something he was not looking forward to, at all. He was trying to figure out why, but nothing logical came to him. He couldn't think of anything he had done wrong, as far as attitude went. He hadn't violated any training rule. "Maybe Coach wants to see if I'm still interested in playing, now that I know I'm not starting this game. He's had trouble with seniors not starting in the past," he thought. He told himself that he was not going to be one of those trouble makers. No way. His dad would roll over in his grave if that happened.

He knocked on the door. Coach was working on a practice plan at his desk.

"You wanted to see me, Coach?"

"Yes, Jeff, come on in. Here, sit down." He showed the senior a chair next to his desk

"Thanks." He sat down and folded his hands on his lap, anticipating the next step.

"Jeff, are you upset that you're not on the first unit?"

"Well….yeah, not at you or Coach Smith or anybody else. Just at me. At myself. I know I could do better. That's all." He dropped his head, a bit disappointed.

"It's a long season, son. I've never really taken much stock as to who starts the first game. I'm more concerned as to who will still be around starting game nine or our playoff run. That's far more important to me."

"But, Coach, it's Valley Forge. Our home opener. And Brad Brown. Coach, I wanted to be out there for that."

Coach Reynolds eyes twinkled a bit. "Don't worry. I don't think you have any reason to doubt that you won't be out there next Friday night. Jeff, for our team to go as far as it can, we are going to need our seniors to come through. Especially the ones who come off the bench or are back-ups. Now, I've always admired the way you prepare. You have the respect of both the coaches and your teammates. Not many others on this team have what you have."

Jeff raised his eyes a bit. "Thanks, Coach, but, in my mind, with all due respects, the best way I can contribute is not by being on the sideline leading cheers. It's being on the field. I want to be on the field making plays, helping Hillsdale win. So I have to keep pushing." His voice cracked a bit.

"I agree. Let me ask you a question, Jeff."

"Okay, go ahead."

"What would you say if I told that I can guarantee a way for you to be on the field?"

"Coach, you know me. I don't want any preferential treatment."

"You're not going to get any. I'm asking if you want to be on the field."

"Of course. Certainly."

"Good. I'm naming you special teams' captain. You will be on the punt, punt return, kickoff, Starburst return, and extra point and field goal teams. I am holding you personally responsible for making sure those units not only perform well, but also become a strength of our squad." A pause as Coach Reynolds let it sink in. "Do you think you can handle the job?"

Jeff's eyes lit up. "Think I can? Oh, Coach, I KNOW I can. You won't have to worry about a thing."

Coach said, "Jeff, most people don't know that over 20% of high school games involve some phase of the kicking game. Your units will be held accountable for all of the hidden yardage that's out there."

Jeff was getting excited, squirming in his chair. "Coach, you don't know what this means."

"Oh, yes I do. I just put a guy in charge who will help us win football games."

A voice interrupted over the speaker phone. "Coach Reynolds? Coach Reynolds?"

"Yes."

"Please come to the office immediately. Mr. Hubbard needs to see you right away."

"Okay. I'll be right there." He turned to Jeff. "Be ready to lead the team in stretching this afternoon with the other captains. I'll inform the team. When the special teams' period begins, you lead them."

"Thanks, Coach." He extended his hand.

Coach Reynolds took it and shook it warmly. "Congratulations. I'm counting on you."

Jeff Fairchild nodded and turned away, skipping out of the locker room door. "See you this afternoon."

Coach Ben Reynolds smiled, turned and trudged up the short flight of stairs and headed towards the office. "I wonder what he wants this time."

August 20

Chapter 36

"Dammit! Where are my damn sunglasses?" Bubba Brown reached all over in his front seat, trying to locate his sunglasses. The sun sitting in the eastern sky was virtually blinding him as he drove along Main Street in Valley Forge. It was just at the right level to bring new meaning to the term "sun block."

His search was fruitless, so he held his hand up in front of his face as he approached the traffic light, the only one Valley Forge possessed. He couldn't really see the color of the signal, but he decided to slow down into the intersection, just to be safe. Looking side to side, he couldn't really notice any oncoming traffic, so he chose to drive straight through. The white Jeep Cherokee from the north didn't appreciate his decision and let him know it with a series of long beeps from its horn.

Bubba didn't slow down, however, and just kept going. He waved to the driver, almost mockingly, and continued on towards the high school. He was supposed to meet with Brad's counselor this morning. This lady had called him a few days ago concerned about Brad's schedule. It seemed as though Brad needed to make some changes so that he could complete all of his graduation requirements. When he asked Brad about it, his son said nothing back. In fact, Brad hadn't really spoken to him since the night he had come home drunk.

Brown rubbed the spot under his eye where his son had hit him. It was still a bit tender, but at least the swelling from the black eye had gone down. The guys at work didn't believe him when he told them he had run into a door; he never told his friend Joe anything about it, since he hadn't seen the mechanic since that night. When he met Helen for dinner the other night, she just tossed her head, figuring that she didn't really need to know. He had tried to apologize to Brad the next afternoon when he came home from practice, but his son just shrugged his shoulders with a "Huh-rumph!" and turned to the stove to begin making macaroni and cheese.

A casual glance in the rear view mirror revealed that Bubba was being followed. The change in sunlight made it difficult for Brown to see what kind of a car it was. "Now, who in the hell is on my ass this early in the morning?" he wondered.

The sudden flashing of red lights gave him his answer.

Bubba pulled his truck over as the police car followed him. He waited for the officer to come to his window, trying to locate his wallet. He remembered that he put in the visor before he left that morning. When he lowered the visor, the wallet landed on his lap, followed immediately by the missing sunglasses. "My lucky day," he muttered.

"I'm Officer Chambers. May I see your driver's license, sir?" a voice sounded.

"Good morning to you, too, Officer." Bubba tried to sound friendly, hoping it would help, as he handed the policeman his license.

He looked at the picture on the license. "Mr. Brown, do you have an insurance card?" Bubba reached for his glove compartment as the officer took a step back.

"No need to worry, Officer, I got it right here." He handed the card over, smiling that toothless grin again.

"Mr. Brown, I got you running that stop light at the corner of Main and Henry back there. Do you know that you almost got in a wreck?"

"I couldn't see cuz I couldn't find my damn sunglasses. I didn't see no light, no car, nothing. I was like blind, you know. I didn't mean no harm."

"I'll be right back, Mr. Brown." He turned and returned to his squad car. Bubba sat in silence, contemplating his fate. He began to think of as many excuses he could to try to get out of this ticket. Sick kid at school. Naw, he wouldn't believe that. Color blindness. No chance. Spilled his coffee on his pants and didn't respond in time. That would be good, except he didn't have his coffee yet. Had to go to the bath-

---

"Mr. Brown, how long have you had this truck?"

"Over ten years. Why?"

"I ran a check on it and the report said it's supposed to be red. A red 1995 Chevy pick-up truck."

"I had it painted a while back."

"How long ago?"

"Couple three weeks. Why?"

"Just making sure it's yours. Had some car-jackin' going on lately."

"Yep. She's all mine. This don't look like a truck anybody'd steal to you, does it?" Bubba laughed.

The policeman took a long look at the broken down truck. "Nope, can't say it does. Here's your papers back, Mr. Brown.

Thank you, Officer."

"And here's your ticket for running the light. Court date and your options are on the back. You'll need to sign here, Mr. Brown."

He handed Bubba a pen and a mini-clipboard. Bubba reluctantly signed his name and took his copy. He stuffed it above the visor.

"Be careful, Mr. Brown. Have a nice day." With that, Officer Chambers strolled back to his squad car.

Bubba Brown grabbed his sunglasses and smashed them on the dashboard.

August 20

Chapter 37

Jason Stone was running late, much to his dismay. The last thing he needed, though, was a speeding ticket, especially since he was meeting his cousin Tony Chambers, a county deputy sheriff, for breakfast. Explaining a screw-up like that would be rather difficult.

He slowed down as he approached the only stop light in Valley Forge. This was the second time he had been to this little town in the last month or so; before it had involved the initial investigation surrounding the Hillsdale case. He didn't really learn too much during that first visit; having Tom Thomas along prevented him from really digging into areas he thought he should. Thomas just wanted to talk to the school officials, and, as usual, they just reiterated the same lines they had heard before, as if they rehearsed them from a play.

"Yes, we have a student enrolled named Brad Brown."

"Yes, he has residency in our district. Both his mother and father are listed on the forms."

"No, we have no knowledge of any improprieties (*one of those 'intelligent' words school officials like to use*) regarding his transfer.

"No, we do not know the Nortons. No, we don't know Coach Ben Reynolds. We are very satisfied with our head coach, Coach Buchanan *(like anybody really cared)*."

"No, we have had no dealings at all with Mr. Bubba Brown."

Statements like those just led Stone to believe that much more information was available if the right people were asked. Thomas, on the other hand, was genuinely pleased with these answers and aborted the trip right after they left the school office.

Jason believed something was coming down in the very near future, and things didn't appear good for Hillsdale. Both Thomas and Mr. Phillips had tightened up even more during their daily briefings. The last one just yesterday was significant in that the subject was not even discussed. The two seemed intent on taking action without Jason's support or knowledge; they acted like he wasn't even there. So, when he told the secretary, Judy Watson, that he was going to be gone all morning foe a doctor's appointment, nobody raised any eyebrows.

The fact was Stone, with a little help from Tim Hallion, was now convinced that Bubba Brown was involved up to his ears in something, but it may not necessarily be in the Reynolds/Hillsdale case. They were both sure that the case he was connected with mainly was the hit and run accident which put Julie Reynolds in the hospital. The problem was they had no proof.

He asked to meet his cousin for breakfast in hopes that somebody in the law enforcement field in this area might be able to come up with something. He knew that all of these local law enforcement guys had been on the alert, but sometimes there could be blurbs or views behind the scenes that don't always get public. Besides, his cousin owed him a meal from the last time the two of them had gone golfing. Taking money from Tony was always easy.

Jason pulled into the first stall across from the door of *The Warrior's Shield*, obviously a local hang-out similar to *The Cabin* in Hillsdale. He noticed a squad car with water dripping from underneath, telling him that his cousin had just recently arrived.

"Hey, Tony, you have to run the AC this early in the morning? Isn't that wasting the taxpayers' money? Shouldn't you be out arresting criminals or something?" Jason said jokingly as he approached the booth where his cousin, Officer Tony Chambers, was sitting.

"Maybe," Tony smiled, 'but, at least I'm comfortable when I'm working," slapping Jason on the shoulder. The two men were more friends than family. Their history went back all the way to Little League when they played on the left side of the infield together.

"Besides, I just got done bustin' a guy for runnin' a red light. We got one light in town, and he says he can't see it.

He must think I'm nuts or something," Tony said, looking through the menu.

"Yeah, I was worried I was gonna get a speedin' ticket coming here. You know how I hate to be late."

"I know. But this guy, with the heap of junk he was driving, he's no threat to any land speed records. Bubba.... Bubba Brown...in his nasty black Chevy pickup." He chuckled in that deep, baritone voice which always made Jason giggle.

Stone stopped short. "Bubba? Bubba Brown?" He couldn't believe his sudden good luck.

"Hmm, hmm." Chambers nodded. "I seen him around town some before, but his truck was red then. Liked to spend lots of time watching the football boys from the parking lot. They say his boy is one tough football player. Hadn't noticed him lately, but that's because he changed his truck color."

"How long has that been? Did he say?" Jason asked eagerly.

"Couple of weeks or so, I guess. Hey. Let's get something to eat. I'm starving. Remember, Buddy, my turn to buy today."

Jason opened his menu to the omelets. He chose the biggest one on the list, with all of the fixin's. His reasoning was two-fold. First, he needed to get some more information from his cousin. Second, and more important, anytime he could spend his cousin Tony's money, he was going to take full advantage of the opportunity.

"Listen, Tony, I'm working on this case for the State, which just might help you guys too. Where would a guy in Valley Forge go to get his vehicle painted?"

August 20

Chapter 38

The feedback from his "apology blog" had been extremely encouraging, yet "Rocco" still wasn't satisfied, nor happy. Subscriptions to his site had increased, posters had been increasingly supportive, and business was booming, to say the least. Yet, with less than a week to go before the season opening football games, Tim Hallion still wanted answers. What was going to happen to Hillsdale?

Anything?

Nothing?

A slap on the wrist?

Suspensions?

Firings?

This much he knew; the quieter it had become from the state in the past few weeks, the more he was sure a ruling was going to come any day now. He did not want to be scooped on the story, but he wasn't going to take any chances in publishing any type of rumor.

"Fool me once, shame on you; fool me twice, shame on me," he had said to himself time and time again since his last trip to Hillsdale. Hallion was convinced of several things. First, like Jason Stone, he felt very strongly that Bubba Brown was smack dab in the middle of the Julie Reynolds hit and run. All factors pointed that way; the time of day, the direction he was traveling, the craziness when he left the parking lot, the fact there's a back road in that area that goes to Valley Forge. Just the other day, he read online that Julie Reynolds, who originally had been unable to recall much from the accident, remembered that the color of the truck was red. Hallion couldn't figure how the cops just didn't move in and arrest Bubba Brown. That would suit him and a lot of others just fine!

Second, he felt that Hillsdale was going to get nailed. They shouldn't; he knew that, also, but deep down inside, he reasoned that this eerie quiet from the State office was the "calm before the storm." They had some piece of information which nobody knew about, and that was going to be the telling blow.

Finally, he was convinced that somebody in this area had set Hillsdale up for the fall, and, for the first time, he had narrowed his list of suspects to from five or six to just one. It had taken a great deal of time to figure this out, but, after sorting, deciphering, analyzing, and studying more than thirty possibilities, Hallion was able to eliminate the improbable and settle on the probable. However, again he had no proof; he had no facts that connected this person at all to the case; he had nothing to base it on, other than the fact that this individual had a reason, a motive, and the opportunity.

He had spent the last day and a half figuring out a way to connect his suspect to the case. It finally dawned on him that he should use his chosen field as a means to an end.

He had been waiting for a response from an e-mail he had sent to a friend of his who worked for AOL. He knew this friend would send him the information he needed.

"Ding! You Got Mail!" Hallion spun in his chair and clicked.

August 20

Chapter 39

"Hi, Coach! Good to see you again!"

Ben Reynolds was taken aback a bit as he entered the school office. Two of the last people he had expected to see that day were Reverend and Mrs. Norton, especially in the principal's office. The trio had not been in the same room alone since that night back in March at *The Cabin*, when all of these supposed violations had taken place.

"Hello Mrs. Norton, Reverend Norton. Good to see you both again, although this is a pretty strange place to meet," Ben smiled.

"I agree," Mrs. Norton said sharply in reply. "Coach, let's cut to the quick. Why are we here today? Is there going to be some trouble?" Reynolds was glad to see she hadn't changed much. Caustic as ever.

"Priscilla, take it easy. None of us are happy about being here. Don't take your feelings out on Coach Reynolds," Reverend Norton retorted.

"William, this never would have happened if he hadn't brought that laptop to the restaurant," she snapped.

"Scilla! That will be enough! You apologize to Coach Reynolds right now!" her husband scolded.

"No need, sir!" Ben interrupted. "Mrs. Norton, I'm sorry for all the stress this has caused you, us, the school, everybody. But believe me when I tell you, I have done nothing wrong. WE have done nothing wrong. Everything is going to be all right, I promise. You'll see."

"I've prayed very hard for justice," Mrs. Norton said, fighting back tears. "God will help us find justice. Coach, I'm just very frustrated, very stressed. I'm sorry."

Reynolds began to walk towards the lady to offer support when the door of the conference room opened, and Alton Hubbard, the principal, and Jon Robbins, the Athletic Director, both entered the office. Their facial expressions pretty much told the story. Trouble.

"Thank you all for coming. Please follow us. We have some concerns to discuss. The State has sent us its decision," Hubbard said blandly and turned towards the door he had just exited.

Robbins added nothing, just leading his hand towards the door, showing them the way. The three shaken individuals followed and proceeded to chairs around a large rectangular table. Slowly, each of them slid into a chair and began to fidget. Glasses of water sat in front of each person. Mrs. Norton was first to drink, but the two men quickly followed.

Coach Ben Reynolds had been nervous before, but it always had been replaced with anxiety and excitement.

These emotions were normal before every game for the veteran coach, and when the opening kickoff occurred, the feelings left as quickly as they had come. This experience was different. He was nervous, sure, but it was accompanied by fear. His hands broke into a sweat, and, even though he had just gulped a glass of water, his throat was parched.

"I'll just read the fax we received," Hubbard said. "It comes from the State Athletic Association office.

Dear Mr. Hubbard:

On July 24, this office received an official complaint against Hillsdale High School and Head Football Coach Ben Reynolds. The accusation stipulated that in March of this year, Mr. Reynolds knowingly and willingly met in a public restaurant with Reverend William Norton, his wife Priscilla, and their son, Jack. At this meeting, Coach Reynolds showed the family a video highlight film of the Hillsdale Hillmen football squad from the prior season...

"A highlight film! They must be crazy!" screamed Coach Reynolds.

"Coach, please let me continue," Hubbard responded.

....from the prior season in hopes of luring the Norton family to leave the community of Willow Brook and enroll at Hillsdale for the upcoming season.

This office, headed by state officials Tom Thomas and Jason Stone, has gathered information from witnesses in Willow Brook, Hillsdale, and Valley Forge. The latter was included when allegations involving the role of former Hillsdale resident William "Bubba" Brown, his wife Helen and his son Brad were made, which were subsequently dismissed when no pertinent connections to this case were found.

Citing State Code #51.1 which states, 'No school official, staff member, or personnel shall willingly contact a student from another school district with the intent of convincing that student to transfer into their school district,' this office has determined that Hillsdale High School and Coach Ben Reynolds are GUILTY of illegal recruiting in the case of Jack Norton.

Citing State Code #51.2 which states, 'No student shall willingly become in contact with one school district while he is enrolled in another school district,' this office has determined that Jack Norton is GUILTY of illegal contact.

Mrs. Norton rocked in her chair, sobbing into some Kleenex she pulled from her purse. Reverend Norton appeared to be praying, Ben Reynolds felt his hair on his neck standing on end.

This office has determined the following punishments to be enforced today, August 20:

1)   *Hillsdale High School is on probation for one year. Hillsdale High School must present in writing within*

thirty days a comprehensive plan that targets the coaching staff of Hillsdale High School and the pitfalls of recruiting. All coaching staff personnel must sign off on this plan for the plan to be valid.

2) Mr. Hubbard and Mr. Robbins are to attend two workshops at the State office between now and December 20 concerning the rules of recruiting. Failure to complete these directives as stated within the time frame given will result in suspension of membership from the State Athletic Association with a non-participation status for ALL of the State tournament series for one calendar year.

3) Jack Norton is declared INELIGIBLE to participate on any athletic teams of Hillsdale High School. However, should he decide to return to Willow Brook High School, since he was in good standing when he left, he would be allowed to participate in any sport, provided he meets all of the guidelines for that sport. For this to happen, Jack Norton must enroll at Willow Brook High School by August 23.

4) For his willing involvement in this case, Coach Ben Reynolds is declared SUSPENDED for six months as head football coach. He is NOT to have any contact with his players, his coaches, his staff, or anybody connected with the football program during this time.

Any further incidences involving Coach Reynolds and illegal recruiting practices will result in his permanent removal from all coaching possibilities in this State.

As listed in our State by-laws, any or all of these decisions can be appealed to the Governing Body. Those appeals must be in writing and in this office within 48 hours. A hearing date will be set as soon as reasonably possible, once the written appeals have been received.

We are indeed sorry to have to take this action, but the actions of the parties involved and the information we received gave us no choice. The integrity of the State Athletic Association must be upheld.

Sincerely,
Monty Phillips
State Athletic Association Executive Director

Hubbard folded the fax and set it in front of him. Robbins rose and filled the glasses again, but nobody drank.

Priscilla Norton continued to cry softly. Her husband came to her side and rubbed her neck. He continued to whisper prayers as he massaged her.

Ben Reynolds continued to fume in his chair. He gripped the arms extremely hard, squirming from side to side. He was furious.

"They want a fight? They picked the wrong man this time," he muttered to himself. His face was beat red.

August 20

Chapter 40

He couldn't remember the last time breakfast had tasted so good. Not only was the omelet scrumptious, Jason Stone learned that Valley Forge had two auto body shops that also did custom painting. His cousin, Officer Tony Chambers, at first was suspicious and reluctant to share any information. He couldn't see the need to involve Jason in this case; after all, the police had already talked to both places, or at least tried to. However, Jason convinced him to share some basic information because he told Tony the State needed to investigate anybody and everybody. This was a critical factor in **their** case.

The first one, *Rudy's Body Molding,* looked at the police like they were crazy. They only dealt with cars, and expensive ones at that. They had given up working on trucks over twenty years ago. The other place, *Valley Forge Auto Repair,* was owned by an eccentric old coot, Joe Josephson. When the police tried to question him, he just quoted the 5th Amendment and refused to cooperate in any way, shape, or form. The sheriffs didn't push the issue much; Valley Forge never was a town where folks pushed things too much.

Jason felt today he would get some answers…finally. He drove by *Rudy's*, but did not bother to even stop. Everything his cousin had told him about that place was true. They didn't do trucks.

Valley Forge Auto Repairs, however, was another story. As he approached from almost a block away, Stone thought he was entering the world of Fred Sanford of *Sanford and Son* fame. Car parts and body scraps lay all over the place with no rhyme or reason to the pattern. The "office" was nothing more than a broken down house trailer, while the main work area was a long, metal shanty covered by a tin roof. Nothing about the place indicated any organization or style. Two dogs lay on their bellies next to a smoldering barrel. It smelled like rabbit to Jason as he got out of the car. He smiled, "Yep. That's got to be him."

A spry, yet disheveled man with white hair approached him. He wore a drab pair of bib overalls with only one of the straps attached. His t-shirt looked as though he hadn't changed it in days. Jason noticed a familiar gray stubble on the face which dripped beads of sweat, telling him that this man had been hard at work for awhile that morning.

Joe Josephson squinted at the young man who stood next to his fancy SUV but couldn't make out the face because of the glare. "Good morning, sir? What can I do for you on this beautiful morning?" he said, cheerily.

"Never make the first or third out trying to go third."

"What did you say?" Joe queried.

"When you see a pitcher for the first time, remember he hasn't seen you either."

Joe took a step to the side and got a better look at his visitor. A huge smile came to his face. "Jason. Jason Stone. How in the Sam-Hell are you?" He slapped Stone on the shoulder and grabbed his hand.

Jason returned the handshake. "Hello, Coach. You always said when you retired that you wanted to become an autos guy. I thought you and your wife moved out to Arizona, though,"

"We did. She left me out there. Got involved with our UPS driver. He took that ad 'What can 'Brown' do for you?' a little too seriously. Caught him 'unwrapping a package' once, if you know what I mean. Then she blamed me and my work hours for the whole deal. So they ran off together. Didn't have any friends out there, so I came back to the Midwest. Got this place cheap. Don't make a lot of money, but it keeps me busy."

"Coach, remember when you used to tell me about my Uncle Randy and all those hours in the batting cage? I never forgot those words. I use them to motivate me all the time."

"Good. Glad to see at least somebody listened to me once in awhile. Your uncle was the best student of the game I ever had. The hours he would put in….You were good, too, but Randy, well, Randy was something special."

Jason was immediately sorry he had brought it up, but he knew he needed an ice breaker.

"Sent me some Cub tickets earlier this summer, your uncle did. Three rows from the dugout. Sat right by this wacko lady, Sara Davidson. Said she's been comin' to games for over seventy years. Boy, she could cuss a blue streak, too."

"He sent me some, too. I got to sit out by the bull pen." It was a lie, but Jason wanted to at least hold his own with his former baseball coach.

"So," Coach Joe said to change the subject, "what brings you here today? Surely, you don't need that car of yours fixed. No offense," he chuckled, "but it's a bit too fancy for this place."

"No, Coach," he grinned back, "nothin's wrong with my car. I came here because I need a huge favor. I think you can help me out."

Coach Joe Josephson listened intently as Jason Stone relayed the whole story, starting with his connection with the State Athletic Association, to the Bubba Brown-Ben Reynolds fiasco, to the Nortons and their dilemma, and also to the hit and run accident involving Julie Reynolds. Jason remembered from his baseball days that the coach liked to spit on the ground a lot when he was interested in a story. The more Stone talked, the faster the coach spit. He was exceptionally active during the hit and run story.

"Coach, we think the guy who hit Mrs. Reynolds lives in this town, drove a red pick up truck that day, and since had it painted. Have you had anybody in here getting a paint job like that in the past month or so?" Stone purposely omitted Bubba Brown's name.

Josephson turned and walked away, scratching his chin. He had a choice to make now. When the cops came earlier, he had brushed them off, because he didn't want to get involved. He was relatively new to Valley Forge, and he didn't want any type of publicity. Even though he had gone drinking a few times with Bubba Brown, he really didn't know the man very well, and he certainly didn't trust him one bit. Brown appeared to be a guy out for himself. Joe never did believe that story about the tree, but he never had reason to connect him with any real type of hit and run. Until now.

He spun quickly around and gave Jason the answer he was looking for. "Not only did I do a paint job on a red truck, I remember the name of the guy who had it done. Your friend from Hillsdale, Bubba Brown. Said he hit a tree, but I always thought he was lying. The bumper I banged out and smoothed over. That crappy truck is more rust than anything. We've had a few beers before, but I never trusted him that much. Say, I just remembered; we're supposed to go out tonight after work for a few."

Jason had a plan. "Coach, I think it's time we go to the bullpen and put out the fire. A little hit 'n run of our own. Are you game?"

August 20

Chapter 41

"Bingo!"

Tim Hallion's AOL friend had come through. Some strings had been pulled, but Hallion had struck gold. He had his connection.

He had his friend trace all of the cell phone calls made by Mark Lowery over the past three months. The State had no record of the call because it came over the line as an "Unlisted Number." Hallion had known the number himself from all of the times he had contacted Lowery in the past, but the recent developments had raised his suspicions. "If Lowery had lied to me, and if what Coach Reynolds had said was true, then it stands to reason that Mark Lowery would be perfectly capable of being the instigator of this whole mess," he reasoned.

So he played a hunch. Jason Stone had given him the time of the original phone call, which indicted the Hillsdale people since state officials documented that part. An e-mail message to his friend Jake Flowers had done the rest. Flowers was a long-time friend and fellow classmate from

Northtown. They had played football together, side by side in the secondary. Flowers intercepted four passes his senior year, not quite as good as Hallion's five. As a duo, though, they raised lots of havoc for opposing receivers and quarterbacks in their league.

Since high school and college, they had gone their separate ways, but they had always stayed in touch. In fact, Hallion had been godfather to Flowers' first child, a boy he and his wife had called "Rocky" in honor of Tim's web site. Jake Flowers had worked for AOL for over ten years and rose steadily up the corporate ladder. Getting the information for his friend Tim wasn't too hard, especially after Hallion had explained the reason behind it.

Tim Hallion had figured correctly that Mark Lowery was the person behind the initial contact call to the State. This e-mail message proved it. Flowers had provided a list of all of Lowery's phone calls on his cell and the times those calls had been made for the past three months. The phone number from Lowery's cell matched the one received by the State on July 13 at 9:40 AM.

He felt exhilarated for a brief moment. A little digging on his part had given him some vital, meaningful information. Then he thought, "OK, what do I do with this? There's been no crime committed. All Lowery did was set the Hillsdale guys up, using another guy's name, to boot. The State was stupid enough to think he was telling the truth. And now look at what we got."

However, Hallion had made Coach Ben Reynolds a promise. The last thing he wanted to do was disappoint that man again. He had to come up with a way to smoke out this rat and have him get what's coming to him. Sometimes, he felt, to deal with rats, you have to think like a rat.

"Of course!" he exclaimed. "This could be exactly what he deserves."

August 20

Chapter 42

Ten minutes had elapsed since the Nortons had left. Mrs. Norton finally stopped crying long enough to announce that she couldn't understand how a merciful God could allow something like this to happen to her son, her family, and their good name. She started to blame everybody again, but her husband stepped in, just like he did before, so she wouldn't get herself into any more hot water. The two left arm in arm, muttering something about moving back to Willow Brook, but no one really paid much attention to it.

For his part, Coach Ben Reynolds hadn't really moved since he first heard the news, other than to call his wife. As he expected, Julie was livid; she wanted to hop in the car right then and there and drive down to Monty Phillips' office and let him have it. She also vowed they would get the best lawyer money could buy, just to make "that bastard" pay for causing this embarrassing shame. She also wanted to call the radio station and newspaper to give them an official statement from the family before they got a hold of the news themselves. Then, just as quickly, her voice mellowed, and she said she wanted to tell their children before they heard the news from somebody else.

Not once did she sound like she was in tears; not once was there any sign that she wanted to give up without a fight or throw in the towel. In fact, she never did say to Ben, "I'm so sorry," or "I feel bad for you." The last thing she said before she hung up was, "Don't worry, Ben; you're the Coach. We'll beat this, just like we've beaten everything else." Just one more reason why he loved her so much.

Hubbard and Robbins were just sitting in their chairs, waiting to see what the Coach was going to do next. Reynolds spun around suddenly in his seat and began to rise. "Where are you going, Coach?" Mr. Hubbard asked.

"I've got things to do," came the stern reply.

"Sit down, Ben." Alton Hubbard rarely called anybody on his staff by his first name. His gentle, yet firm tone told Reynolds he should listen. He sat back down and looked the principal right in the eye.

"Ben, I don't, …we don't," indicating Jon Robbins, "like this any more than you do. But we have to abide by the ruling….as least for now."

"Why? You both know we got screwed."

"Yyyyyes, we dddid, Cccoach," stuttered Robbins, "bbbut we got to do what's rrrright."

Ben's eyes narrowed, and he leaned forward in his chair. "What's right is that we tell Phillips to go ____"

"No!" Hubbard shouted. "No! That's not how we do it. More importantly, that's not how *Coach Ben Reynolds* would do it." He paused. "We all know that."

Reynolds' gaze rotated from Robbins' to Hubbard's face. He slumped back in his seat, and rubbed his chin. "So, what do I do?"

Hubbard replied, "The first thing you do is to contact your coaching staff and brief them. You have to decide which of your assistants will run the program in your absence."

Robbins butted in. "I ttthink it should be Smmmmitty, but that's my oppppinion."

Hubbard didn't break stride. "Once you get that straightened out, you need to talk to your team. Make them aware of your expectations, the team goals, their responsibilities during this period of adjustment. Understand?"

Ben sat still for a moment, pondering his plan of attack. Getting the coaches figured out was one thing; talking to the kids- well, that would be hard. Really hard.

"I can do it."

"Then comes the hard part, Coach."

"The hard part?"

"Yeah." Hubbard paused and swallowed. "Then you pack up your things and leave. You go away and don't come back until we get this straightened out. You will no longer be the Coach."

Those final words punched Reynolds in the stomach. He rose from his seat slightly, doubling over in the process.

Reality had set in. He fell back into his chair and tried to compose himself.

"Sorry. That's a bit tough to take."

"I understand," said Hubbard, 'but the sooner we all accept that fact, the better it will be for all of us."

"Easy for him to say," Reynolds thought to himself. He struggled to regain his composure. Robbins brought another glass of water. "Ggggggot to be ggggood for sssssomething," he smiled through his stutter.

Reynolds took a deep breath and stared at both men. "I will do what you ask....today. I can't promise about tomorrow....or the next day even." His voice slowly began to increase in intensity. "But, if you think for one minute I'm going to sit here and let some idiot take away my football team, least of all a *lunatic* like Monty Phillips, then you don't know Ben Reynolds! He suspended me without even talking to me HIMSELF??? For six months???? That's crazy! That's crazy!!! This is MY team! And NOBODY else's! Do you hear me?" His voice thundered through the office.

Hubbard waited a few moments to let the coach's panting subside. "You feel better? Now that you have let it all out." His tone was cold. "Doesn't change anything."

Ben began to stammer. "Alton, what am I gonna do? What will people say? I'm no no no cheater. I didn't DO anything." He put his head in his hands.

Robbins spoke up, calmly and without his traditional stutter. "Coach, you do what you've done every year you've been here. You do what's right!" He slapped the table.

The coach peered through his fingers, as his hands slid down his face. His voice regained its coach-like demeanor. He slowed down and spoke assertively. "Okay, like I said, I'll cooperate....today. But, I want you to make an immediate appointment for me to meet with Mr. Monty Phillips and that Council, or whatever it's called. I want an official appeal filed right away. Today! I believe I have the right to meet this man face to face. The sooner the better."

"Okay. We'll set it up. Once we get it, Jon and I will go with you, nobody else. No family. No lawyers. The fewer people who go, the greater chance we will have to try to persuade him to see our side. Agreed?"

"My wife will want to go along," Ben insisted.

"I don't think that's wise, but I understand. While you talk to your coaches and players, I'll handle things from this end."

Alton Hubbard stood. Jon Robbins followed. Finally, Coach Ben Reynolds rose to his feet. He extended his hand to first the principal and then the athletic director.

"Thanks, fellas," was all he could muster. Slowly, he turned and shuffled out the office door, his broad shoulders sagging somewhat. Hubbard and Robbins remained standing as the door closed behind him.

August 20

Chapter 43

...August 20...11:00 a.m. ...For immediate release to all media

Rocco's Rocks to Honor Area Radio Legend

Rocco's Rocks is pleased to announce the winner of the first ever 'Friends of High School Football' Award. This honor will be bestowed annually to an individual who has contributed greatly to the cause of promoting high school football in this part of the state. Criteria used to determine the award will include impact on the game, enthusiasm, loyalty to the area in which the individual lives, displayed spirit, and willingness to share both times and talents, among others. Nominees for the award will include members of the local media, local sports boosters, and, naturally, local fans. Beginning next year, a nomination process will begin through Rocco's Rocks to get the fans of the area more involved.

This year's winner is Mark Lowery, former legendary radio voice of the Hillsdale Hillmen. For over fifteen years, his call

of a Hillsdale football on WZJE radio was captivating to all listeners, and his signature "Touchdown" call was copied by the Hillmen student body and fans alike.

Tim Hallion, owner and moderator of the Rocco's Rock web site will be on hand to present the "Friends of High School Football" Award to Lowery prior to the kickoff of the Valley Forge Warriors–Hillsdale Hillmen football game next Friday night in Hillsdale. Game time is 7:00, with the award presentation set for 6:45.

August 20

Chapter 44

Things were rapidly becoming a blur.

Trying to reach Jack Norton on the phone had failed for over an hour. Ben had wanted to talk to the young man before his parents got a hold of him first, but, by the time Jack answered his cell phone, the 'damage' had already been done. He told his coach that his mother was basically hysterical about the matter, invoking God's wrath on anybody and everybody she knew. Despite efforts to calm her down, neither her husband nor Jack had been able to reach her. The coach told Jack how sorry he was things had gotten so out of hand, how he still believed the young man had done nothing wrong himself, and how they would fight for the principles they still believed in. He told Norton what a solid young man he was, and he closed the conversation by asking Jack for a favor. He asked him to go to his mother and give her a huge hug. "You stay with your family, Jack. They need you now," the coach had said.

The meeting with his coaching staff had been extremely uncomfortable. Jon Robbins sat in on it, first of all, and it seemed to Ben that he was just making sure the head coach did what he had been told to do. The coaches normally met at noon in between practices to plan the next workout. Usually, they went out to get something to eat and bring it back so they could have a working lunch. Practice schedules, which Ben already had printed out, would be reviewed, topics for meetings before practice would be discussed, and any personnel changes would also be handled. It was a routine that this veteran staff had been used to for years, so, oftentimes, the mood initially at one of these staff meetings was light and jovial.

When they came in on that Saturday, though, it didn't take long for them to see that things were about to be different. Robbins' presence alone was one sign, but the blanched appearance of Ben Reynolds was the greater indicator. They sat in silence as the athletic director and then Ben briefed them on the recent developments. Jerry Smith spilled his Coke when Ben asked him to take over the reins, but he quickly regrouped and agreed to the proposal. The other coaches volunteered for every duty under the sun, even those they didn't have the faintest idea how to do. Ben smiled a bit as he listened to their eager concern and then raised his hand to stop them.

"Look, guys. This too shall pass. Until then, run the program the Hillsdale way, just like you did when Julie was hurt. You all have been around here a long time with me, and I have the utmost trust in Jerry...in ALL of you. We always talk about how no one individual is bigger or greater than the team. Nobody, not even us coaches….not even the HEAD coach." He paused for a couple of seconds, letting that last point sink in.

"So here's the plan. I have to tell the players myself at our 1:00 meeting. Most of them probably already know, but I still am going to talk to them. Jerry, I want you to be there when I talk to them. Jake, Brian, Danny, you guys stay in here and get the practices organized. This afternoon's is already in place; then you got the weekend to get ready for next week. It's Game Week, so our routine won't be that much different, but if Jerry wants to make any changes, you guys listen to him as you would listen to me. Jerry and I will get together this weekend to iron out this transition." He turned to Robbins. "Don't worry, Jon, Jerry will come to my house; I won't come around here." Robbins nodded.

Ben then came to the hardest part.. "Men, I'm sorry…. so very sorry…to have to throw this burden on you. Maybe it will work out. I hope to have an appeal heard next week. If I get it and the ruling is overturned, it will be back to business as usual. If not, then it will be up to you to make sure these kids perform to their capabilities. Always have a 'Plan B' ready, just like we talk about. I know you will do your best. I gotta go."

He stood up, quickly shook hands with each of them and headed out the coaches' office door. He paused a moment at the opening. "This could be the last time I ever walk outta here," he thought. He left in a hurry towards his date with his players.

August 20

Chapter 45

"Men, sometimes, in life, we get handed issues and dealings we don't like nor agree with. Today has been one of those days, as most of you already know. The State Athletic Association has ruled that I can no longer be your football coach...., at least for now.....maybe for this season.

"They say I cheated, men; they say I broke one of their laws. They say I tried to recruit Jack Norton to come to Hillsdale High School to play football. They say that "Perfect Fan" DVD, remember the one we showed last year at the banquet? They say that DVD was a highlight film of our successes here at Hillsdale, which is a violation of the state code.

"What's worse, to me, is they also say Jack Norton and his family are cheaters, too. Jack has also been suspended; they're not letting him play for us this season. That's a cruel, unfair blow to that young man and his family because he's a senior now, and they have taken his senior season away from him. That's not fair. Even though he's been here only a short time, I hope that you will have his back and still support him. I just told him on the phone that he's still a Hillsdale Hillman.

"No, none of this is fair! None of it! But screaming about it, or pouting about it, or crying about it will NOT change anything. I'm here to tell you that I am NOT a cheater. I had to come in front of you today and look you in the eyes and tell you that. The thought of my players thinking their head coach is a cheater or a crook is the ONE thing I feared the most. So you MUST believe that!

"I'm also here to tell you that I plan to fight this ruling. I have requested an appeal before the Governing Body, which, hopefully, will be heard next week. If things work out, then this will be over very soon. But, that's my fight, not yours!

"We have to worry about our team, what's best for the team, like we always try to do! We are going to plan for the worse case scenario. My sentence is for six months, and let's assume that's what it will be. What do we do, what do YOU do in the meantime? First of all, let's get one thing straight. You players are going to do what YOU have to do, while I take care of my own business, like I said.

"Coach Smith will now be in charge until I come back…if I come back. I want you to respond to him and the rest of the coaches, just like you would to me. I want you to carry on like you did when I was gone with my wife's issue a couple of weeks ago. You did it then; you can and WILL do it now.

"Men, we talk all the time about what makes Hillsdale football special. It's never been the wins; it's not the conference titles; it's never even been the trips to the playoffs; and it's certainly not the coaches! The *players* have always been the reason we are special. The *players! You!* You *players* buy into our philosophy and principles and then do your best to carry them out. That's what makes us special! We have always told you that no one individual is bigger than the program. That includes all of us-players, coaches, managers. That's especially true now.

"Until I get this worked out, I will not be a part of this season. I will not be at practice; I will not be on the bus going to games; I will not be in that locker room with you; I will not be on the sidelines. Our season, however, goes on. I want you to *promise* me that you will carry on the tradition we have talked about. If I have that guarantee from you, it will make this ordeal I must undergo a lot easier. Do I?"

An uneven chorus of "Yessirs" echoed through the hall.

"When I see you in the halls here at school, I will speak to you; I hope you speak back. When I see you around town, I will speak to you; I hope you speak back. As far as games go, I don't know what I'm going to do yet, but you will have no bigger fan than Ben Reynolds."

A pause. The stillness of the auditorium was broken by several sniffles from various seats.

"Just a while back, I talked to you guys about not letting anything or anybody come between us and our goals. Don't let this. Don't you dare let this."

Another pause.

"I wish you nothing but the best. Now, Coach Smith has a few words he'd like to say to you. God bless you…all of you!"

With that, former head coach Ben Reynolds walked slowly up the aisle towards the auditorium door. Alone. At the door, he stopped briefly as Jerry Smith's words echoed , "Okay men, this is what we're going to do…."

The door closed behind him. Ben Reynolds found the first chair in the hallway he could and buried his head in his hands.

August 20

Chapter 46

Like most Saturday nights, *Barney's* was hopping. Beer specials were combined on this night with Margarita specials, since a local mariachi band was playing live out in the Beer Garden.

Bubba Brown sat in a corner booth by himself and just soaked in the atmosphere. For the first time, really, since he had moved to Valley Forge, he felt like he belonged. And he had his son Brad to thank for that.

Last night, at the Valley Forge Warriors "Fall Extravaganza," which was nothing more than a pre-season, tune-up scrimmage, Brad Brown was, undoubtedly, the best player on the field. From his running back slot, he scored two touchdowns, one of them a remarkable fifty-five run, in which he bowled over two would-be tacklers, spun away from a third, and scampered across the field towards the end zone. On defense, he was everywhere, knocking down two passes, getting two sacks, and recovering a fumble, which he caused by stripping the ball away from one of the junior running backs. This had been his first real experience on defense, and he actually might have been better on that side of the ball.

Bubba just sat in the bleachers with his wife Helen and beamed. He only got excited during that long touchdown run, screaming his son's name as he crossed the goal line. He quickly regained his composure when Brad sent him an icy stare as he jogged by on his way back to the bench. After the scrimmage was over, Warrior fans, both young and old, approached him, gave him "high-fives," and congratulated him and Helen on Brad's performance. "Thanks for moving here" and "Thanks for bringing your son" were repeated much more than once as the stands emptied.

Since Helen had to get back to Hillsdale that night because she had to work this morning, he had waited outside the locker room for Brad after the scrimmage was over to congratulate him, just like he had done before at Hillsdale. When his son finally emerged, the elder Brown rushed up to him and embraced him. "See, son. You see? I told you this would be better! Way to go out there! Way to go!"

Brad merely pulled away from his dad and continued walking. Bubba was puzzled. "What's the matter, son? You were great out there!"

The younger Brown turned and said, "Dad, that defense I went up against tonight was pitiful. *You* could have scored on those plays."

"But not like that! I never could run like you can. That's the stuff scholarships are given for."

"If we play like this against Hillsdale, we'll get killed. Coach Buchanan just got done rippin' us a new asshole in the locker room. He wasn't very happy. Told me I got a long way to go yet. Told me that in front of the whole team," Brad added.

"Aw, that's just his way of motivating you."

"I liked Coach Reynolds' way better," his son replied, turning and heading towards a waiting car in the parking lot.

Bubba's enthusiasm was unfazed. "Don't worry Brad. We'll get 'em. Next Friday night, we'll kick their ass! Up and down the field! You have fun! See you at home!" he yelled.

On top of that, an even better piece of news came his way. Earlier this afternoon, word came that Hillsdale got nailed by the State, and his good buddy Reynolds was suspended for some time. When he heard that news at the gas station around 4:00, he couldn't stop laughing. He crawled back into his truck, pulled down the visor and looked at the worn photograph of Ben Reynolds he kept, all the time laughing fiendishly. Even more reason to celebrate tonight.

He twirled the straw in his margarita and took another sip. "What a great day! Brad's the star and that asshole Reynolds won't be coaching next Friday. An easy win for Valley Forge. What more could I ask for? Boy, am I glad we came here," he said to himself.

Tonight he told Joe that he would meet him here at *Barney's*. He wanted to be by himself and soak in any adulation other customers might send his way concerning

Brad's performance. However, even though he had been there an hour and had already finished two margaritas, not one patron even noticed he was there. "Well, I'll just keep drinkin' till somebody recognizes me," he mused.

"Hi, 'Dad of the Day'!" It was Joe. "Nice job last night. For your kid, that is!"

"Thanks! Yeah, he was pretty awesome. You get to see it?"

"Naw. Had to work late." A second figure emerged from behind Joe's shadow. "Hey, I brought a younger buddy of mine with me. You don't mind, do ya?"

"Not at all." He extended his hand. ""Hi. My name is Bubba Brown."

"Nice to meet you. I'm Jason Stone. I used to play baseball for this guy," motioning towards Joe.

"You did? When?"

"Back in high school. We used to be pretty good up in our neck of the woods."

Bubba punched Joe in the arm. "You never told me you were a coach. I'll be damned. Pull up a chair, both of you. First round is on me. Hey! Bartender! Waiter!"

Joe sat opposite Bubba, while Jason slid into the chair right next to Brown. "Aren't you Brad Brown's dad? Brad Brown, the running back?"

"That'd be me," Bubba grinned.

"Aren't you the same guy who made a big stink and moved his kid out of Hillsdale last spring?"

Bubba took a huge gulp of his margarita, almost draining it. A waiter appeared.

"What'll you have guys?" Bubba asked, trying to rapidly change the subject. "Margarita specials and beer specials tonight.

Joe broke in. "Give me a draft."

Jason spoke with a purpose. "I want a High Life. A Miller High Life."

"Bring me one more of these," Bubba added, holding up his goblet. When he did, his eyes met Jason's hard stare.

Stone continued. "Well, aren't you the guy who moved out of Hillsdale?"

Bubba tried to fend off the questioning. "Maybe. What if I am? Who are you anyhow? Who is this guy, Joe?"

"He played shortstop for me way back. He played next to a guy named Tony Chambers. He's a cop, you know."

At the mention of the policeman's name, Bubba's fingers slipped off his glass. He tried to remain cool.

"Hmphh! Don't know him." The waiter appeared with the drinks. He set them down in front of each of them. "Put it on my tab, pal," Bubba said.

Jason slowly took a drink from his clear bottle. "They say the 'high life' comes to those to work for it. Is that why you moved to Hillsdale, Bubba?"

"I think I've heard enough. Joe, this punk's an asshole. I'm leavin'."

"Not yet." Stone grabbed his arm and squeezed it. "Bubba Brown, I know lots about you." Bubba sat down.

"I know all about your argument with Coach Reynolds. I know all about why you came to Valley Forge. And I know something else nobody else does."

Brown started to squirm. "What's that?" he asked looking at both Stone and Josephson.

"I know why you got your truck painted black," Jason whispered very slowly, and then took a swig from his bottle.

Bubba took a deep breath of relief. "Oh, is that all? Just ask Joe here. He talked me into it the night after I hit a tree and banged up my bumper. That's no big deal!" He took a gulp from his drink and set it down.

Jason didn't let up. "That's what you want people to believe. I know for a fact that you had been in Hillsdale that morning; that you got shut down in that restaurant *The Cabin* by a high school kid; that you drove off like a bat out of hell down the road towards Wal-Mart; just about the same time Julie Reynolds' car was coming from the other direction; and here's the biggest one." He leaned forward right in front of Bubba's face. He whispered very clearly. "I know you are the one who hit her car and then took off down a gravel road back here to Valley Forge. That's what I know." He leaned back in his stool and took another drink from his beer.

Then he stopped and stared a hole right through Brown. "You want to know somethin' else? I'm lettin' the cops know."

Bubba Brown's mouth was agape. Suddenly, he rushed from his seat, knocking a tray of drinks out of the hands of the waiter who had served them.

"Hey!" the man exclaimed. "Get back here!"

Brown kept on moving through the crowd. He was certain both Joe and Stone were hot on his heels, but he never turned around to check. He bolted out the door and raced to his truck.

Inside, Jason Stone text-messaged on his cell phone, "The rabbit is loose." He closed his phone and took another swallow. His high school baseball coach looked at him and said, "That was very impressive. A very impressive performance from the bullpen." The two men rose from the table, dropped off two twenties at the bar for all of the drinks, and headed to the parking lot.

"At least, we can take care of his bill," Jason smiled as they walked outside.

August 20

Chapter 47

Bubba Brown's heart was racing. He quickly found his keys and turned the ignition on. It was dusk, and the glare from the setting sun was right in his eyes. He came to the edge of the parking lot, paused as he looked both ways, and squealed out into the roadway.

"How did that asshole know all of that crap? Who was he, anyway?" he thought as he drove away. "I shouldn't have left, but I don't need to hear that crap. I thought Joe was my friend, that asshole. Bringin' guys like Jason Stone around. Well, he can't prove anything. Nobody saw me."

He hadn't gone a quarter of a mile when flashing lights appeared again in his rear view mirror. "Oh, no, not again," he moaned. He thought about trying to lose the squad car, but quickly dismissed the idea. He pulled off to the side of the road and, once again, tried to find his license.

A familiar voice greeted him. "Good evening, Mr. Brown. Remember me? I'm Officer Chambers." The margaritas began to rise in Bubba's throat.

"What now, Officer? There wasn't a red light this time."

"No, not a red light, but there is a stop sign at the exit of the parking lot at *Barney's*. You never stopped. Plus, you squealed your tires. Not only that, Mr. Brown, but I've been looking for you. I got some information about you from a friend of mine. I heard you were in Hillsdale the day Mrs. Reynolds' car got it."

Bubba started to get out of the truck, but Tony Chambers stopped him in his tracks. "No, no, no. no, Mr. Brown. You stay right there. Or maybe you would like get out. Maybe you would like to take that little walk down the white line out here. It doesn't take any time to set it up. Just how long have you been at *Barney's* anyways?"

Bubba slumped back in his truck. He was sweating profusely. "What do you want, Officer?"

"Just the truth, Mr. Brown. Were you in Hillsdale that morning?"

Bubba said nothing, resigned to his fate. He reached for the visor and pulled it down. He grabbed the faded picture of Ben Reynolds and spit on it one more time. "You bastard!" he muttered under his breath.

"Okay, Officer Chambers" he screamed. "I can't take any more! I give up! I'll tell you everything about that morning...."

From the parking lot over a quarter of a mile back, two figures stood together near the stop sign at the exit of the lot. Jason Stone and Joe Josephson smiled as they saw the flashing lights twirling in the evening sky.

August 20

Chapter 48

The last group of visitors had just left, and former coach Ben Reynolds and his wife Julie were cleaning up all of the glasses and pizza boxes. The late afternoon and evening had consisted of a steady stream of well-wishers and supporters who stopped by to offer encouragement to the Reynoldses. Their pastor, fellow teachers from Hillsdale High, fellow real estate agents in town, friends and neighbors, former players, and even media people dropped in to attempt to lend a helping hand in any way they could. Of course, there was nothing anybody could really do, so they mainly just talked about the old times, the better times, and what to look forward to in the upcoming days.

Julie and Ben tried to be polite to everyone, but really what they wanted was some time to be alone and think this matter out. Ben had always found strength and common sense in Julie's advice. He had used her ideas on more than one occasion when the situation warranted.

For her part, she hadn't even had a chance to be alone with him to just share the emotions of the day yet. She knew that her husband had been extremely strong-willed that day, and she was bound and determined to make sure he wouldn't let up. She wanted to discuss their strategy for next week's hearing. Alton Hubbard was hoping to finalize the details of the meeting, which was tentatively scheduled for Wednesday. They were all surprised Monty Phillips responded today. It was if he had expected them to appeal and was waiting at his office for a phone call.

No matter, they would fight this like they had fought so many battles before. Early money problems when they first got married, the year they had spiders all over their house, followed by three successive nights of bats flying around their bedroom, the spring the twins got measles at the same time, even this most recent episode of her traffic accident; all of these were handled together. Not to mention all of the problems being a head coach. This would be no different.

"How are you holding up?" Julie asked.

"Got a bad headache," Ben responded. "Way too many people and way too much fuss."

"They love you, Ben. They're in your corner. They want what's best for you." She put her glasses down and snuggled up to him, wrapping her arms around his waist. "So do I."

He kissed her on the forehead. "Thanks. I know. Tomorrow, after we get a good night's sleep, I want you to help me plan what I'm going to say for the appeal."

"Piece of cake," she said. "We'll have those guys eating out of our hands before this is over. They have no case. That DVD was nothing."

"You know that. I know that. Everybody around here knows that. But, *they* don't know that. The people in the State office, the ones who make the call, *they* don't know that. That's our one and only hurdle. We have to be ready."

"Ready? Ready for what?"

"We have to be ready in the event they won't listen. My decision to retire may come earlier than we had planned."

She buried her head in his chest.

Part 5

August 24

Chapter 49

Alton Hubbard had spent the entire weekend in conversation with Monty Phillips and the State Office. Fortunately, on Monday, Tom Thomas sent Jason Stone to Hillsdale to work out all of the details for the appeal. In less than two hours with Stone, Hubbard and Athletic Director Jon Robbins knew the time, the place, who <u>should</u> come, who <u>could</u> come, and, most importantly, the format for the day's proceedings. On Monday afternoon, the three men called in Ben Reynolds to brief him as well.

Ben was given the option of bringing a lawyer with him. On the surface, that initially seemed to be a good idea, but Ben dismissed it because he did not want to appear intimidating before the Governing Body. No, he felt that he could handle matters himself.

The format for the day was simple. The "hearing" was scheduled to begin at 9:00 a.m. The only representatives Hillsdale chose to bring were Mr. Hubbard, the principal; Mr. Robbins, the athletic director; Ben and Julie Reynolds; and the Nortons, William, Priscilla, and Jack. As of Tuesday night, the Nortons had not decided if they were going to appeal their phase of the ruling themselves or not. Mrs. Norton strongly believed that God would provide the answers for their family in due time. However, they did agree to accompany the rest of them, in case the board members had any questions directed towards them.

The Nortons were the last to arrive at the State Office. Jack had to be excused from school for that morning, so his parents insisted that Hubbard ask the panel if they had any specific questions for Jack right away. That way, he could turn right around and head back to school thirty miles away. He had a chemistry exam that afternoon.

At 8:55, the Hillsdale contingent entered the huge conference room. In front of them was a dais with seven empty chairs behind the huge table facing them. On either side was another small table with just one chair at each. The Hillsdale group sat down at another huge table up in front of the dais. Alton Hubbard chose the middle seat. Jon Robbins took his to Hubbard's immediate left, flanked by the three Norton family members. Ben Reynolds sat to the right of the principal, with his wife Julie right next to him. Notebooks, files, and briefcases were shuffled around as preparations were finalized. Ben felt very uncomfortable in his long shirt and tie. He really didn't want to dress up, but Julie felt it important to display a "professional image." He tugged at his collar.

Promptly at 9:00, a side door opened, and a group of nine people entered the room. They slowly made their way to their seats on the platform. A young lady took her place to the table's right, obviously a secretary to record the proceedings. At the single table to the left, Ben recognized Jason Stone, one of the original investigators who had come to Hillsdale.

At the head table, Ben only recognized Tom Thomas, that little weasel who had come with Stone that first day. None of the others he knew. They had to be principals from various high schools around the state. A total of five of them took their seats and placed name placards in front of them, so their names would become visible. One man, however, remained standing, Mr. Monty Phillips, the Executive Director.

Monty Phillips stood about six feet tall and weighed around 175 pounds. He wore round wire-rimmed glasses on his thin, narrow face. He had a receding hairline, and he had combed what was left of his hair straight back. To Ben, he couldn't have been much more than forty-five years old, and he did not appear to be a very menacing figure. In fact, if Ben hadn't seen him in this set of circumstances, he would have sworn he was a "nerd." He wore a dark blue suit with a shiny yellow tie.

"Good morning. My name is Monty Phillips, and I call this meeting of the Governing Body to order." He pounded a gavel. "This morning we are gathered here to address an appeal from Hillsdale High School, regarding this office's ruling on the suspension of Coach Ben Reynolds, the suspension of Jack Norton, and the contingency plans given to Hillsdale High School in the wake of our ruling. This stems from the investigation and collection of evidence this office compiled and the subsequent ruling it made surrounding the illegal recruiting tactics used by Hillsdale High School and, specifically, Coach Ben Reynolds, regarding Jack Norton, a former student at Willow Brook High School and currently an enrolled student at Hillsdale High School."

With that, Phillips, who, Ben felt, must like to hear himself speak, spent the next ten to fifteen minutes reviewing all the pertinent state codes examined, those in his judgment which were violated, the penalties for each, and the justification for the ruling he had made. Halfway through his dissertation, Priscilla Norton interrupted him, wanting to know if there was any need today for the board to ask Jack Norton any specific questions. If not, she wanted to send him back to school to take that test she was worried about. Phillips appeared miffed, but she was insistent they decide immediately. "I'm sorry, sir. But my son's education comes before this 'dog and pony' show," she told them. Jack was sent on his way.

Once he was finally done, Phillips asked the board members if they had any questions so far. None being heard, he turned his attention to the table in front of him. "Mr. Hubbard, will you introduce your party?"

Hubbard went down the line, starting to his left. Each member stood and smiled to the board members, but they just sat there stone-faced. Only Jason Stone acknowledged them with a nod at each introduction. "This is not going to be easy," Ben thought as he sat down.

"Do you have a statement, Mr. Hubbard?" Phillips asked.

"Yes, we do, sir.

Hillsdale High School has always maintained high standards in its dealings with its students, its community, and the State Association. Our reputation among the other member schools in the Midwestern Conference and the immediate area schools is impeccable. We have done our best to run a First Class operation in everything we undertake.

We strongly believe that the punishments given our school, Coach Reynolds, and Jack Norton, are both unfair and unreasonable. During the investigations headed by Mr. Thomas and Mr. Stone, we were extremely cooperative and kept nothing secret about our motives and our actions. After talking to Rev. and Mrs. Norton, the two of them noted that it was extremely apparent that nobody was hiding anything. All of us have been extremely open and honest with our information and our principles. In no way, do any of us feel we have violated any state mandate.

Rev. and Mrs. Norton met with Coach Reynolds at a public place. No conversation was made regarding promises, guarantees, or endorsements regarding athletics and Jack Norton. Jack has even told the two gentlemen he barely even spoke that night to Coach Reynolds because his mother had all of the questions. A DVD was shown; we have freely admitted that. Yet, in no way is that DVD representative of what an athletic highlight tape would consist of. Instead, it is a tribute to the moms of last year's squad and the memories they should have of the relationship they have enjoyed with their sons.

Hillsdale High School sees the ruling made by Mr. Phillips and the State as a personal attack on the integrity of our school. We totally oppose this ruling and ask the indulgence of the Governing Body in this matter.

Hubbard folded up the statement and put it back in the folder. He folded his hands and added firmly, "We are willing to discuss this matter and answer any further questions you may have." Ben was proud of Alton Hubbard. He had saved his best moment for now.

Monty Phillips addressed the board members, "Is there any of our Governing Body who would like to ask Hillsdale a question? Any comments on what you just heard?"

Nothing. Not one word. Not one peep. They just sat there like zombies, blank looks on their faces.

Phillips addressed the group. "It appears that the Governing Body has no questions at this time. Unless you have something else to add, I believe we will adjourn and discuss this matter in private."

"Wait a minute," Ben Reynolds stood up. "I'm the one who asked for this hearing. I believe it's within my rights to address this group, especially you, Mr. Phillips."

He stood behind his chair and pushed it in, not even giving Monty Phillips a chance to respond. He left his notes in the briefcase. "I really, for the life of me, do not understand why we are even here today. But if my fate is going to be decided by someone, I want that person, or that group, to look me right in the eye and pass that judgment. The people who interviewed me, questioned me," he waved his hand towards Stone and Thomas, "are not even the people making the judgment on my fate.

He turned his attention to the State's Executive Director. "Mr. Phillips, we have never talked, never met; I never even knew what you looked like until I saw you this morning. Yet, you take information, you interpret evidence, and then you draw a conclusion which affects my reputation and career, without even talking to me personally? You never once asked me for my side of the story in a one-on-one conversation! I never knew that's how justice is done in this state.

"If you had done that, if you had taken that initiative to bring me in, sit me down, ask me the same type of questions Mr. Stone, who I thought was very thorough, and Mr. Thomas did, and then pass judgment, I might be able to live with this better."

"Which of you principals here this morning, if you have a student sent down to the office for discipline, doesn't sit that student down and let him know exactly how you feel and what his status is? Same with a teacher. If you have an evaluation or a matter of explanation with a teacher in your own district, don't you gather information and then bring that teacher in before you reach a judgment? Isn't that treating people right?

"Not here. Instead, we get, *I get* innuendos, rumors, and false information that tarnishes not only my reputation, but also that of the school I work for. We were given no timetable for this verdict we were handed, no warning that it was about to come; what we got last Saturday was a fax or an e-mail detailing our fate. Is that how professionals are treated?"

He was surprised at how calm he had been during this entire delivery. Not once had he lost his composure.

"I'll tell all of you the truth, face to face, man to man, so you can hear it from me. Yes, I met the Nortons. Yes, we talked about school. Yes, I told them to contact our school office to get particulars. No, we never discussed the benefits of playing sports at Hillsdale High School. Yes, I did show them a DVD on my computer, which was nothing more than a four-minute tribute set to music to our mothers from last year's football squad. The Nortons were concerned that, with the size of our school compared to theirs in Willow Brook, kids are a number, not a person, and that people in our community don't care for one another. Mrs. Norton has said she was unimpressed and quit watching thirty seconds in. No, this is NOT a highlight tape. THIS is a highlight tape."

He walked over to this briefcase and pulled out a copy of the prior year's highlight video. He held it up for all to see.

'This is our highlight DVD. It is over 60 minutes long. If you want to watch a really good high school football highlight tape, I recommend you sit down and watch this one. It's really well done. That other one, as I said before, is only four minutes long. It was not even included in the original copy, but some of the parents wanted it added on as a PS on the end.

"I went to *The Cabin* that night because Reverend Norton asked to meet with me. Think about it. If I were going to recruit a young man, why would I choose the most public place in Hillsdale to meet with his family? Why would I risk my career and reputation by showing them a highlight video in a public restaurant? That makes no sense."

Finally, someone spoke up. A middle-aged heavy-set Italian from the suburbs offered his thoughts. "Wait a minute. Do you really expect us to believe that you never once tried to convince this kid to come to Hillsdale that night?" A quick look from Phillips silenced him.

"Sir," Ben smiled, "with all due respect, you were not there. The parties who *were* there have all told you the same thing. Nothing went on that night that deserves the "death sentence" we have received. Nothing went on to deserve any type of punishment, if you ask me."

"I came here today because I firmly believe in my principles and my ethics. I also believe in the Norton family and Hillsdale High School. This situation should never have come to this point. But it has. I wanted to speak to you, Mr. Phillips, face to face. I have done that. I am hoping you extend me the same courtesy. Do you have anything to say to me in response?"

Monty Phillips looked at his Governing Body members and slowly rose to his feet. "It is the policy of this Governing Body to listen to the information given and then go into Executive Session to discuss the matters and announce its ruling and any changes it may chose to make.

"At this time, this appeal is now concluded, and the members will adjourn to the chambers. Thank you everyone for your input this morning. Once we have reached a decision, we will notify you immediately. We hope it won't take too long. You may wait here, or in the hallway. Mr. Stone will be our liaison."

With that, he pounded the gavel, and the group slid out the adjoining door, as expressionless as they had been when they entered.

August 24

Chapter 50

Two hours went by, and still no word. The Hillsdale group was growing restless, partly because they were getting hungry, but more so because they were just plain tired of the waiting.

Julie Reynolds was so proud of Ben's performance. "Save that speech," she told him. "you can use it to instill some passion in your players."

"Yeah…if I get the chance," was Ben's reply.

Even Priscilla Norton had been impressed with Coach Reynolds. "Coach, I have to tell you, my husband in his greatest hour could not have delivered a better sermon. God definitely inspired you this day," she said with a twinkle in her eye.

In fact, the entire Hillsdale contingent had been pleased with the way they handled things in the appeal. Hubbard had been firm and assertive, and Ben had just been plain eloquent. Everyone had been really impressed with his analogy involving the student sent to the office and the teacher in a conference. They all agreed that the principals in that panel had to be able to connect with those points.

As the time continued to lengthen, they waffled as to whether the delay was to their advantage or not. Some felt good about it; others were not so sure. What had bothered them was how stoic the Governing Body was, sitting up there with no expression or response, other than one question. Hubbard guessed that's how Phillips wanted it. He had prepped them as to how they should behave, leaving the oratory entirely to him. In fact, the one principal who did speak up probably got reprimanded behind closed doors.

Without a doubt, Julie Reynolds was by far the most optimistic of the bunch. "There's no way we don't walk out of here with a favorable ruling. I just hope they come to their senses back there soon so Ben here can get back to practice. Wednesdays are always big days in the preparation. Last day of contact for the week," she said knowingly. "Besides, we're all getting hungry."

Just then, Jason Stone walked through the chamber door. "Mr. Hubbard, this is for you. I hope you find it all in order." He handed Hubbard an envelope and stood patiently.

Hubbard opened the envelope, read its contents, and dropped them on the floor.

"Appeal Denied."

This time it was Reverend Norton who got angry. "Where are those people? It's time they heard from a man of God." He bolted towards the door, with both his wife and Julie hot on his heels.

Stone stepped in front of them. "It's no use. It's no use. There's nobody in there."

"What do you mean?" Julie asked.

Jason searched for the right words. "This decision was made over an hour ago. They all left immediately after they decided. Except for me, they've all been gone for over forty-five minutes."

"Damn them," swore Reverend Norton.

Part 6

August 26 — Game Day

Chapter 51

Opening game in Hillsdale was not just an event; it was a Happening! Booster Club members began preparations months in advance for this wondrous occasion. Despite the recent summer drought, the field was in immaculate shape. A sprinkling system funded by the Boosters three years ago ensured that Hillsdale High would have the plushest grass around.

Senior players' dads spent each Wednesday night before a home game painting the field. Normally, at most schools, this was a job done by the custodians, but as part of the community involvement insisted upon by Coach Reynolds, they shared the responsibility. Dads and custodians would spend almost two hours painting the yard lines, the hash marks, the sideline numbers, and the decal in the middle of the field. An ice sculptor who worked in town volunteered his services over five years ago to create various stencils to be used as logos for the center of the field. More care was put into that decision each week than any other. In fact, the moms joked that if their husbands put as effort in their yard work at home as they did that field, they all be candidates for "Yard of the Month." After the end zones were finished, the men would clean up the equipment and then head to a nearby watering hole to discuss this week's forecast for the game.

Not to be outdone, the moms went overboard in all of the other areas. Using Styrofoam cups, a weekly slogan was placed in the cyclone fence that surrounded the field for all to read. For this opener, "We Shall Overcome," and "We Love Coach," obvious references to the recent problems endured by the Hillsdale Hillmen, were chosen.

From each of the four corners of the bleachers, a huge gold flag with the green letters "H H" floated in the summer breeze. Streamers in those same school colors danced from the backside of the framework.

The moms also made signs with each of the players' numbers on them and planted them along the curb in front of the school. Green and gold signs were posted everywhere, offering support to this player and that player, and the coaching staff, with more than one saluting Coach Reynolds. They set up "Booster Booths," selling all kinds of Hillmen paraphernalia, including megaphones, bobble-head dolls, t-shirts, and pompons.

The most striking trademark, however, was the aroma that emanated from the renowned pork chop tent. For over twenty years, Don Crowley and Pat Wayman had combined forces to cook pork chops and chicken breast sandwiches, and folks would come from miles around for just for the food. Last season, when Hillsdale hosted South Fork in game eight, the visiting school pre-ordered over 100 sandwiches for the players to eat after the game. South Fork may not have won the game that night (Hillsdale in a romp 47-3), but at least their players ate well afterwards.

It was that aroma that hit Jeff Fairchild's nose as he made his way to the locker room. He couldn't believe the number of people already there over two hours before game time. Tailgaters from both Hillsdale wearing green and gold and Valley Forge in their maroon and white had set up shop in the parking lot, and the cheerleaders were busy peddling those chops and chicken breast sandwiches. Luckily for both sides, neither seemed willing to invade the other's territory in the parking lot. Jeff figured it was too early for trash talking. Of course, the fact that four or five of the Hillsdale police department patrolling the grounds certainly didn't hurt.

Jeff was the first one in the locker room. After school ended, he headed to the cemetery to talk to his dad. While other players were driving around town listening to their music, Jeff always chose the solitude and peace that visiting his dad brought him. Earlier that morning, his mother had placed a picture of his dad wearing his high school football uniform on his dresser before she had to go to work. That was her way of saying "Good luck!" to her son.

At the cemetery, Jeff thought about his coach. It wasn't fair what Coach Reynolds was going through. It wasn't fair to him, and it wasn't fair to his team. Coach Smith was doing his best to get the team ready, but Coach Smith wasn't Coach Reynolds. Jeff was worried that the team's focus wasn't where it should be. So many people seemed to be angry over matters they had no control over. The last two days had been rather wild.

He also thought about his old friend, Brad Brown. The two hadn't talked since Brad had moved, but Jeff was really looking forward to playing against him and stopping him tonight. Even though they had been friends, Jeff was going to get at least "one great hit" on him. He was hoping it would be on a kickoff. He also wondered what Brad's focus would be like. Moving and then playing against his old team was bad enough, but Jeff was wondering how Brad was coping, now that his dad had been in jail since last weekend for being arrested as the main suspect in Coach Reynolds' wife's hit and run accident. That had to be on tough. He remembered how tough it was when his dad died.

But, finally, his thoughts turned to his dad. How he wished his dad could be there tonight watching him play. How much he missed him. This had always been his dad's dream, watching his son play varsity football for Hillsdale. "Dad," he said, "when I go out there tonight for the coin toss as one of the captains, I'll be thinking of you. When I get out there on the field, I hope to make you proud." He had even written the word "Dad" on his game shoes.

He plopped down in front of his locker and looked around. Not one piece of equipment was lying on the floor or above the lockers. Everything had been meticulously put away last night, and nothing had been disturbed. The room, however, smelled sweaty, the sign of a hard-nosed work area. "Good," thought Jeff. "This is the way Coach Reynolds would want it."

He reached into his locker and pulled out for the umpteenth time his scouting report and his offensive and defensive "ready sheets," the papers with all of the information he would need that night. He reviewed his assignments over and over again so that they would become just reactionary. He got up one more time to check the Special Teams depth chart, just to make sure he knew who the substitutes were, in case an injury occurred. He wanted to be ready for all situations.

One by one, the players slowly sauntered in. Nobody said anything. Each player went to his locker to begin his individual preparation. Jeff Fairchild stood in front of his locker and removed his t-shirt. He hung it neatly on a hook and clapped his hands.

It was time to get ready. Game time!

August 26 --- Game Day

Chapter 52

"You can do what you want, but I'm going to the game," Julie Reynolds announced to her husband. "I'm not sitting around here pouting and feeling sorry for ourselves. I'm not giving that butt hole, Monty Phillips, the satisfaction of knowing that his decision changed the way we live. It's Friday; it's Game Day; Hillsdale is going to beat the tar out of Valley Forge tonight, and I'm going to be yelling in the stands, just like always."

She bounced around the kitchen in her green and gold regalia, gathering all of her accessories. Julie wore a summer outfit, a fall outfit, or a winter outfit, based on the temperature and the forecast. Obviously, tonight would be the summer glitz, white shorts with a green and gold polo and green and gold tennis shoes that she had created with a little imagination and lots of paint. She always wore her hair in pigtails with green ribbon in one and gold in the other. There would be no question as to where her loyalties would lie.

For the past two days, she had done as much as she could to pull her husband out of his doldrums. Pep talks, soothing talks, scolding talks--none of that had worked. She tried to fix him his favorite dishes, but he had no appetite. Not even biscuits and gravy had worked.

"For the love of Pete, Ben, why won't you come? You can't let this keep you cooped up forever," she shouted. "Everybody wants you there. Jerry will do just fine, just fine. Those kids need you."

"You go ahead. I may show up later," ex-coach Ben Reynolds answered dryly.

"OK, but don't make me come get you." With that, she went out the back door and drove off in her car, leaving Ben Reynolds alone in his misery. There was no way he was going to that game tonight, or any other game, for that matter. He had attended his last high school football game; he had no desire to show his face in this community publicly.

The last forty-eight hours had been unkind to Ben Reynolds. Besides being shocked and angry over the denial of his appeal, he was even more disgusted and annoyed at the lack of professional courtesy that Governing Body had displayed by leaving before the final results had been announced. What were they afraid of? Public outcry?

Ben Reynolds had not slept since Tuesday night. Oh, he had lain down, but all of the thoughts and repercussions flowing through his head made sleep his enemy. The State had deemed him a *Liar* and a *Cheater*. No matter what everybody had tried to tell him the last two days, those two labels were affixed in his mind. He didn't go to school on Wednesday afternoon, but he had been there the last two days.

On Thursday, he addressed each of his classes and tried to explain what happened with his appeal, but since he couldn't make much sense of it himself, he wasn't sure how convincing he had sounded. At least, he felt a little bit better after doing that

Earlier that Friday afternoon, Hillsdale High School held its first of only three pep rallies during the year. He didn't attend, the first time in over fifteen years he had not introduced the varsity football team to the student body. From his classroom down the hall, he could hear the voices and enthusiasm echoing from the gymnasium, He became exceptionally moved when, all of a sudden, a chant began, "Coach Ben! Coach Ben! Coach Ben!" It gave him chills for a brief moment, but he was too bitter and cold to acknowledge the support by going into the gymnasium.

Liked he promised, he stayed away from the football staff. Jerry Smith had e-mailed him a couple of times, asking where some of the game equipment was, since Ben had handled virtually everything himself on Game Day. He would get the communication head sets ready, medical kit stocked, prepare the video equipment, and organize the clip boards for Stats. This normally took him 30-45 minutes after school.

Today, after school, Jerry had asked to meet him in the locker room so he could get help finding all of that equipment, but Ben refused to go into the area and only told Coach Smith where to look. He had spent the better part of the last hour and a half just sitting in his chair in the family room and staring off into space. Julie called it "pouting." She was probably right.

Six months. It might as well have been six years. Since he had already announced his intention to retire at the end of this current season anyway, there would be no "next game" for Ben Reynolds. His final memory of coaching football at Hillsdale would be Brad Brown fumbling that ball. That's not how he had planned to go out. He was hoping that his last game would be meaningful, with something at stake, a playoff berth or a conference championship game, or the like.

Champ suddenly jumped onto his lap. Ben stroked the back of the dog's neck. Now that his wife was gone, he had a decision to make. Stay home and listen to the game on the radio or go someplace where he wouldn't have to listen to it. Part of him wanted to listen. These were still his kids, his players, coached by his staff, guys he had chosen to teach them the game. But, right now, he couldn't bear to go.

Instead, he hopped in his car went for a drive.

August 26 --- Game Day

Chapter 53

"You're what? You've got to be kidding me."

"Nope. I did. I told them today. Gave them my two weeks' notice."

Tim Hallion adjusted his earpiece of his cell phone so he could hear better. He was on his way to the Hillsdale-Valley Forge game to present Mark Lowery with his award. "But why? I thought you wanted to go up the ladder there."

"I couldn't stand to work another day for those spineless idiots," the voice on the other end explained.

"But, Jason," Hallion offered, "after what you did last weekend, setting up and catching Bubba Brown dead to right, I'd think they would want to pin a medal on your chest. I'm still laughing on how you pulled that off."

"They had no interest at all in Bubba Brown," Jason Stone said slowly and directly. "None. Never did. All they have been interested in from the beginning is putting a notch on their gun belt. All Tom Thomas and Monty Phillips ever wanted to do is make a "name" for themselves. Hillsdale and Ben Reynolds became that notch."

"I thought …"Tim started to say.

"The way they treated those Hillsdale people was brutal," Jason interrupted. "Those people had no chance. None. That appeal was a farce. That Governing Body was nothing but a bunch of puppets, pulled by the string in Monty Phillips' hand. They sat there and said and did nothing. They no more listened to what the Hillsdale people had to say than the Man in the Moon. Phillips had the whole thing orchestrated."

"But I thought you had worked on that. You gathered the information they used," Hallion said.

"I was nothing but a smoke screen. A go-fer. A "do what I want you to" guy. If they had used what I brought them, the case would have been thrown out a long time ago. No, they used that stupid DVD as their prime source of damning evidence. Their ONLY source! They were going to nail somebody, and Hillsdale was going to fall, come hell or high water." Jason's voice was starting to rise.

"That DVD was a highlight tape, wasn't it?

"Bullshit! That was nothing but a music video designed to make moms feel good and cry. Listen to this. This is what put me over the edge. After the Hillsdale folks made their spiel, we all came back into the chamber. Phillips yelled at this one guy for speaking up during the appeal. Then he thanked the men for coming, gave them their mileage checks, and sent them off, sent them home to their schools. We didn't even discuss the matter."

"You got to be crappin' me."

"Then he and Thomas sat down, typed the ruling out, and gave me a copy. He told me, since I was the low man on the totem pole, I was 'selected' to stay and deliver the news to the Hillsdale contingent. He and Thomas were heading to the Country Club for lunch and then maybe some golf. He didn't even have the guts to tell them himself! He made me do it!"

"How'd that go?"

"What'd you think? They were pissed. I was too, but I had to 'play my part.' A bunch of them started to rush the chamber room where we met; that's when I told them nobody was there. That's when they really got pissed."

"Did they do anything? Go after you or something?"

"No. I told them I was in their corner. But that whole thing was just brutal. I apologized over and over, but I don't know how much good it did. I think the principal understood, but the Nortons—the preacher and his wife--- I didn't know they knew language like that." Jason laughed a little.

Tim was worried. "You didn't mention Coach Reynolds or his wife."

"I don't remember her doing much. He just sat there in his chair, staring straight ahead. He looked devastated. Looking at him—that's when I decided to quit. If that's what our State Athletic Association is supposed to do to people, then I don't want any part of it."

"So you quit."

"Yep. When I told Thomas today, he was surprised, almost shocked. He couldn't understand why I was upset over what happened. He said, 'That's how we do it here.' Good, well, they can do it without me."

"So where you going now?" Tim wanted to know.

"Just driving around. Don't have any plans really."

"I'm heading to Hillsdale. Remember, I got that award to give before the game tonight to Mark Lowery. The game ought to be pretty good, too, what with Coach Reynolds not coaching and Brad Brown starting for Valley Forge."

"Yeah, I want to see that award. That ought to be good. When you doin' it?"

"6:45. You can make it. We'll go out after the game. Maybe I can talk you into working for me."

"Yeah, sure. OK. See you in a little bit. I'm about a half hour fro Hillsdale."

"Be careful," Tim laughed. "No tickets. I hear Officer Tony Chambers is on duty here tonight."

"Screw you. See you at the game."

August 26 --- Game Day

Chapter 54

Bubba Brown made sure he wasn't speeding or coming close to running any stop signs or red lights. Traveling down that same back road he taken the day of the hit-and-run gave him an eerie feeling, but he knew it was the quickest and smartest way to get to the game on time.

He owed his wife Helen a lot. She had come up with his bail money earlier this morning after scraping together some cash from her relatives out west. She told them she needed it to help Brad out. They both rationalized it as a somewhat true statement. Brad *had* been worried and bothered for the past three or four days, with his dad in jail and all. The truth was he was upset because he was embarrassed over the whole arrest issue and angry because it was Coach Reynolds' wife.

Brad told this to his mother. He never came to visit Bubba while he was in the county jail; never called; never did anything. He told his mother how he felt only because she kept nagging at him.

Nevertheless, Bubba knew he had to be there for Brad at this game. This was why he had moved; this was why he got that crappy apartment; this was why he and his wife had made so many sacrifices the past five months. Tonight was the night they would show Hillsdale and Reynolds what they had lost.

He looked at the red cut-off shorts he was wearing. It wasn't maroon, but that and his white t-shirt was all he could muster for Valley Forge school colors on such short notice. It sure was different from the green and gold he was used to wearing all those years. But it felt so good.

He wondered how many Hillsdale people he would run into that night. He promised himself that he was going to keep a low profile. No repeats of the incident at *The Cabin*. The more he thought about it, the more he decided to wear sunglasses and a ball cap. Odds were people who might recognize him would remind him of his recent problem. "No use adding fuel to the fire. Get there, shut up, go to your seat and enjoy the game," he thought.

After they won tonight, though, he was going to stop by and have some "Victory Pie" at *The Cabin*. They always had a pie special after home games; the "Victory Pie" slices were always just a little bit bigger. Too bad he would enjoy it more than the Hillmen fans. "Let them eat cake!" he said to himself for no apparent reason.

He told Helen he would meet her in the bleachers. He pulled his black pick-up truck into the parking lot and settled in next to vans all decked out in maroon and white streamers. He put his hat on really low and placed his sunglasses on his nose.

211

He slowly exited the truck and began to make his way through the parked vehicles towards the ticket booths. People were streaming alongside, so he blended in rather easily. After about 100 or so yards, nobody had noticed him. That all changed after he passed a parked Buick.

"Hey, Bubba! Long time, no see. How was your weekend?" It was Joe Josephson.

Bubba responded the best way he knew how. He looked both ways to see if anybody was watching, and then quickly flashed a popular digit towards Joe. He then kept on walking.

"Hey, that's right. I always thought you were Number One, Bubba!" Joe laughed.

August 26 --- Game Day

Chapter 55

His pre-game routine was almost over. All that was left was applying the "No-Glare" strips under his eyes. Everything else was in place, his pants and jersey were snug, his gloves were folded underneath his belt, and his pads were in perfect symmetry.

Jeff Fairchild stood in front of the mirror and applied the strips under both eyes. With each methodical step he had taken, an additional adrenaline rush flowed into his body. No more questions, no more rehearsals, no more practices, no more "ready sheets" to study. It was Game Time, and Jeff Fairchild was ready.

He held his shoes in his hands, the word "Dad" written on the outside of each one. Nobody was allowed to put his shoes on in the locker room. Coach Reynolds didn't want anybody slipping and falling like Hubert Jones did back in 1989. Jones knocked himself out like a light and couldn't play in the game that night. Ever since then, Coach had established a "shoe area" right outside the locker room before the long hallway that led to the field.

Coach Smith entered the room. Jack Norton wearing his jersey and blue jeans stood next to him. "Men, give me your attention." The players all sat still in front of their lockers.

"Now I'm no Coach Reynolds. I don't pretend to be a great speaker or anything like he is. All I know is this. We have gone through a lot together. We have worked very hard in the summer, in the pre-season, and in the prep for this game. Whether Coach Reynolds is here or not, that doesn't change who we are and what we stand for. We are the Hillsdale Hillmen and this is our field. Nobody comes to our field....and takes it from us......Nobody! From the opening whistle until the final buzzer, we are going to rock those Valley Forge Warriors and make them wish they had never gotten off the bus. Brad Brown? Let's give him a homecoming he'll never forget.........Let's make Coach Reynolds and Jack Norton proud.....Are you ready?

"Yes sir!" they cried in unison.

"Are you ready?" he asked again.

"Yes sir!" came the louder reply.

"Are you ready?" he shouted.

"Yes sir!!!!!!!"

"OK. Shoes on, Captains lead us out."

In the hallway, it was amazing how quiet it got again as the players put on their shoes. The four captains worked their way to the front of the group. Jeff stood there with Jake Lewis, Matt Gerard, and Mitch Lupinski, the other captains. They quartet joined hands and waited for a signal to start walking. "Lead us out, Rudy!" Mitch said to Jeff.

They walked through a long tunnel of well-wishers on their way to the gate which opened up to the game field. The players stared straight ahead, reciting in unison "Team" with every other step. As the fans yelled support as they walked by, Jeff's head was spinning. He knew this was going to be a fantastic rush, but he had no idea how awesome it would be. Twenty yards from the field, the captains broke into a little trot. The other players followed suit. As they jogged through the gate, the PA announcer yelled, "Ladies and Gentlemen. Here are YOUR Hillsdale Hillmen!!!"

The roar from the Hillsdale faithful was deafening.

At the opposite end of the field, the Valley Forge Warriors were going through their warm-ups. Number 25, Brad Brown, never raised his eyes as the Hillmen took the field.

August 26 --- Game Day

Chapter 56

For over an hour Ben Reynolds drove up and down the streets of Hillsdale. He had no plan, no destination in mind, just getting away from it all. He gassed up once and thought about heading out of town when he saw the sign for *The Cabin* and decided to stop in. He really hadn't eaten much since Wednesday morning, and he knew there wouldn't be too many people inside, since the game was getting ready to start.

He parked his car and paused for a moment in the lot. He could hear the echoes resonating from the high school field. The Marching Hillmen were performing; he could hear the drum line executing its routine. As he was walking from his car, he could hear the National Anthem being played. He looked at his watch. "Hmmmm. 6:35. They usually play that right at 6:50. Must have some special thing goin' on or something."

When he walked in the door, the bell chimed and he noticed the sign posted "Please Seat Yourself." He walked over to the nearest booth by the window and got comfortable.

He was very happy, since he was the only patron in the building. It didn't take long for him to get waited on.

"Coach Reynolds! It's good to see you," Rachel Sawyer said warmly, as she placed a glass of ice water in front of him.

"Oh, hi Rachel," Ben tried to sound polite. "What are you doing here? Why aren't you at the game?"

"I got called in at the last minute. Kristin was supposed to work, but she got sick today at school. I'm the only one here; I get to be waitress and chef till after the game." "That's too bad!"

"Yeah, well, I need the money if I'm going to go to college."

"You got the grades. Can't you get any scholarship or grant money?"

"I don't know where to go about finding out. None of my family has ever gone to college. All my folks said is if I want to go, I got to earn it myself."

"You stop by my room next week, and I'll show you a few tricks, okay?" He smiled. "Maybe we can make your life a little bit easier. By the way, didn't you play basketball last year?"

"Yes, I did, Coach. But that was then. Work comes first now."

"Rachel, take it from me. You only have four years of high school to enjoy and do the things you want. You got the rest of your life to work. You'll never get these days back again. If you want to play basketball, I can help you figure out a way," Coach explained.

Rachel pulled out her order pad and immediately tried to change the subject. "Have you decided what you wanted yet, Coach?

"Ummmmm. Bring me a BLT and an iced tea with lemon, Rachel."

"Be right back." She turned and went behind the counter and then back into the kitchen, leaving the former head coach alone with his thoughts.

Ben let his mind drift off into the world of nostalgia. He started thinking of all the players and coaches who had served under him through the seasons. He remembered the pep rally from two years ago when he got the entire student body to do the "Wave" in rhythm. He recalled the first coaches' meeting he had with Jerry Smith. Those moments brought a slight smirk to his face.

"What are you thinking about, Coach?" Rachel interrupted him as she set the iced tea down on the table.

"Oh, nothin'. Just rememberin'. That's all."

"Coach, can I sit down a minute? There's something I want to say to you."

"Sure. Have a seat."

Rachel Sawyer flopped into the booth and took a deep breath. "Coach, what happened to you, you know, with the State and all. That was wrong. That was real wrong," she said earnestly.

"Thank you, Rachel."

"No, Coach, you don't understand. To the people here, you're special. You're their coach, their football coach. You always have been. I've heard 'em say so. In here. In *The Cabin*. Lots of folks. They're all behind you."

Reynolds slowly folded his hands on the tabletop. "Rachel, that was before. I'm not the Coach now. I was once the coach, but the State says I'm not now."

She looked him right in the eye. "Once a Coach, always a Coach. You can't turn it off that easily." She paused. "I know why I'm not at the game. Why aren't you there?"

He had no response at first. "I don't know. I guess I'm still in depression a little. I didn't think they'd want me there. I don't want anybody to think I'm a liar or a cheater."

Sawyer smiled back at him. "Every day, Jeff Fairchild comes in here and talks about you. Almost every customer the last few days and weeks has talked about you. All Jeff says is how much the team misses you. 'Coach Smith is good, but he's not Coach Reynolds,' he's said two or three times a night. You should be there, Coach. You should be there for your players."

Ben Reynolds slapped his hand on the table. "Rachel, you know something, you're right. I would not be true to myself if I stayed away. I may not be their coach on the field, but I can be their Number One fan." He stopped. "I got a problem, though."

"What's that?"

"My BLT."

"Don't worry," she said. "I'll eat it. I haven't had supper yet."

Ben looked at his watch. Almost seven. "Here's five bucks. Put it towards your college fund," he said with a twinkle. He placed the bill in her hand and started to get up.

"After we win, Coach, be sure to come back for some "Victory Pie." Dutch apple a la mode tonight. They smell really good back there."

Coach Ben Reynolds stood at the door. "We'll see. Hey…..thanks a lot." He nodded and raced towards his car.

Rachel Sawyer began to clean up the booth. "Glad that worked out. How could I tell him I burned his toast and screwed up slicing the tomato?" she said to herself.

August 26 --- Game Day

Chapter 57

Ladies and Gentlemen. Please direct your attention down to fifty yard line in front of the bleachers for a special presentation. Let's have a warm Hillsdale Hillmen welcome for the owner and sponsor of the Rocco' Rocks web site, Tim "Rocco" Hallion.

A polite round of applause greeted Tim Hallion as he stood in front of the standing room only crowd at Hillsdale High School. Along the fence down by the thirty yard line stood his friend Jason Stone, who nodded when the two made eye contact. Standing next to him on the field stood the guest of honor, Mark Lowery. It was the first time Lowery had set foot back on the high school premises since he had been replaced at the radio station.

Tim Hallion was raring to go. He picked up a portable microphone and addressed the huge throng. "Good evening sports fans, and welcome to the opening game between the Valley Forge Warriors….." A huge cheer erupted from the far side…." And the Hillsdale Hillmen…"A thunderous roar ensued.

"It gives me great pleasure tonight to present the first ever 'Friends of High School Football Award.' Each year, with your help, *Rocco's Rocks* hopes to recognize those worthy individuals who have made their mark in the greatest game ever---High School Football.

"This year's first winner is a legend in these parts. For over fifteen years, Mark Lowery provided the listeners of WZJE radio one of the most thrilling, fun-loving broadcasts of high school football on record. His enthusiasm for the game, his love for the Hillsdale Hillmen, and his loyalty to this community make him an extremely worthy candidate for this award. Let's see who remembers what he used to say when the Hillmen scored a touchdown. Are you ready... one...two...three..."

On three, Lowery virtually grabbed the mike from Hallion and led the Hillsdale faithful in "Touchdownnnnnnn Hillmennnnnnn!" He waved the mike in the air as the crowd roared its approval. Lowery was really eating this up.

Hallion took over again. "But, Ladies and Gentlemen, that's not the only reason we recognize Mark Lowery tonight. There's another reason he is so deserving, another reason he is a true friend of high school football. Most people do not know that earlier this summer," he paused for dramatic effect, "Mark Lowery disguised his voice and called the school officials of Willow Brook High School to tell them that Hillsdale High School and Coach Ben Reynolds was trying to recruit Jack Norton. That's right," he held up a series of papers in his hands, "I hold in my hand a copy of his cell phone records."

A murmur rumbled through the crowd. Lowery made a few faces, but he had no place to hide.

"And not only that, he then called the State Athletic Association with the same claims. These records show his cell phone number was used at the times those calls were made. He even tried to drag Bubba Brown down with him by making it look like he was the one who made the calls.

"Ladies and Gentlemen, this Friend of High School Football, was the instigator in the investigation which resulted in the suspension of Coach Ben Reynolds and the probationary period for Hillsdale High. Let's hear it for this year's winner, Mark Lowery!"

The last sentence never became audible as a raucous chorus of boos rained down on the field, followed by a series of volatile threats. Hallion turned towards where Lowery had been standing.

The former radio voice of the Hillmen was sprinting towards the exit gate, yelling at the top of his voice, "You bastarddddd! You bastarddddd!" He kept running as hard as he could into the parking lot to find his car. As he turned one corner, he knocked down a fan entering the game. He didn't stop to check on the condition of the person he slammed into, but just kept on going. Nobody ever heard from Mark Lowery after that night again.

Coach Ben Reynolds picked himself up, brushed himself off, and wondered what all of the commotion was about.

Reynolds thought the culprit looked like Mark Lowery, but everything happened so fast, he wasn't sure. He began to pursue the guy, but decided if he did, he would miss the opening kickoff, so he chose to enter the gate. The ticket takers let him pass.

August 26- --- Game Day

Chapter 58

Most opening games of the football season are normally high on emotion and not so high on execution. This game, although it was played very hard by both teams, was not an artistic display. Both teams fumbled on their first possession, and neither squad garnered a first down during the first quarter.

The intensity displayed by both squads, however, rivaled that of a late-round playoff game. On the opening kickoff, Jeff Fairchild sprinted down his lane, zeroing in on the Valley Forge return man to make that "big hit" he dreamed about, when he was suddenly decleated by a Warrior missile, Number 25 Brad Brown. Brown planted his facemask right in Fairchild's chest and sent him reeling head over heels backwards. Brown got up chuckling, while Jeff stumbled to his feet, gasping for wind and trying to shake the cobwebs out.

He made it to the sideline just before he collapsed to the ground. The trainer laid him on his back and slowly raised his legs. In a couple of minutes, he got his breath back. He shook off the trainer and focused his eyes back onto the playing area. "I'll find 25 before this game ends," he vowed.

The hitting continued as both squads fought for field position. Jerry Smith's defense stifled the Valley offensive attack. Brad Brown might have had the game's first Big Hit, but he was a marked man when he ran the ball. Whether it was an inside zone run, an outside stretch, or a counter, Brown attracted a crowd every time he touched the ball. Four or five green jerseys and gold helmets swarmed him, punishing his every attempt for yardage. Early in the second quarter, after another futile attempt, he slammed the ball to the ground and screamed, "Block somebody, dammit!" The subsequent fifteen yard penalty for Unsportsmanlike Conduct earned him a seat on the bench and the facemask-grabbing wrath of Warrior Coach Jim Buchanan. His ledger at that point read, "12 carries, 20 yards." He was clearly frustrated.

Hillsdale wasn't much better. Quarterback Phillip Richards fumbled the snap and lost the ball on the first play from scrimmage. From there it went downhill for the most part in the first half. Valley Forge's blitz package confused the blocking scheme of the Hillmen, resulting in several tackles behind the line of scrimmage. When the Hillmen tried to pass, Richards kept getting pressure from the Warrior linebackers, so he never had his feet set when he threw. The Hillmen receivers were able to break free from the Valley Forge defenders, but the quarterback just couldn't get them the ball.

From his spot along the fence in the north end zone, Ben Reynolds was having a heart attack. Even though his good friend, Kurt Hayes, who had joined him once he settled along the fence, did his best to settle him down, Reynolds was having a very hard time staying put. He wanted to jump the fence and sprint down the sideline and take over the offense. It wasn't that Jake Mays was calling a bad game. The young coach, who had played for Ben over twelve seasons ago, had just been thrown into the fire, and he had only called offenses for sophomore games. This was his first varsity game, and he was having a hard time staying ahead of the blitzing defenses.

Ben had always taught his coaches and his quarterbacks that the secret to production was the ability of staying one or two plays ahead of the defense. "Running when they think we're passing, and passing when they think we're running gives us balance. Balance is the key to offensive success," he had always stressed. Mays had run the ball on four consecutive first down situations, with little or no luck. Reynolds wanted to scream out to him to throw a play action pass or a screen on first down, but he was way too far away to be heard. But that didn't stop him from yelling, despite Hayes' efforts to muffle him.

Right before halftime, another blitz from Valley Forge resulting in former Coach Ben Reynolds almost having his heart come up to his throat. Backside pressure from a Warrior linebacker on a third down pass attempt forced the second fumble of the first half by Richards. To make matters worse, the ball popped up into the air into the waiting arms of Brad Brown who scampered thirty yards for the game's first touchdown. On top of that, Richards lay prone on the field for several minutes. When he finally responded to treatment, and came to his feet, he carried his left, non-throwing arm gingerly as he walked off the field. Reynolds knew it was a shoulder problem.

Across the way, in the Valley Forge cheering section, Bubba Brown was beside himself. He jumped up and down screaming, "Attaboy Brad! Attaboy!! Wheee! Awesome, man; that's awesome!!!!" He high-fived anybody and everybody around him, including his wife Helen. He got so excited he nearly fell down. In the process, his sunglasses dropped underneath the bleachers. He was so giddy he hardly noticed.

Halftime turned out to be the worst part of the evening for Reynolds. Since he was standing near the concession stand, many of the Hillsdale fans on their way for refreshments noticed the former coach standing there and made a special effort to stop by and wish him well. He politely acknowledged each slap on the shoulder with a nod, each "Hang in there Coach" with a smile, each "We still love ya' Coach" with a wink. Deep down inside, however, he wanted to crawl into a hole and hide, far, far away from all of this attention. He wished he could disappear from all the commotion. To him, the issue wasn't him, not now; it was the game, and only the game. After a bit, he diverted attention by walking towards the Valley Forge side of the field. At least, all they did was stare.

Coach Smith may not have been as eloquent as Coach Reynolds in his pre-game speech, but whatever he said at halftime should have been bottled up and sold. The Hillmen found another gear, playing with even a more increased passion than what they had exhibited in the first half. Defensively, they blew up virtually everything Valley Forge tried. Once the Warriors got into passing situations, Smith turned his dogs loose, making life miserable for the Valley Forge quarterback, blitzing him with even more success than the Red team had in the first half.

Once linebackers Matt Gerard and Mitch Lupinski blew through gaps simultaneously and leveled the hapless Warrior QB flat on his back. The crowd "oooohed" its approval, especially when the ball squirted loose and the Hillmen fell on it. That led to the first Hillmen touchdown of the season, a screen pass from back-up junior quarterback Kemper Shule to speedy running back Jake Lewis, a play that covered forty-two yards. The fact that Shule was even in the game came as a result of Richards' injury and the suspension of Jake Norton. However, former Coach Reynolds knew that Shule's athleticism gave him an excellent chance to be a good player, so he wasn't totally surprised by his success. He told Kurt Hayes, "During the summer, this kid did okay. I think we'll be all right at QB this half."

However, the point after attempt failed on a bad snap by the center, and the Hillmen still trailed 7-6.

Jeff Fairchild was none too happy with the play of his special teams. They had done nothing so far to contribute to this game. However, that changed on the next possession. First of all, they did a decent job on the subsequent kickoff coverage, tackling Brad Brown on his own twenty-three yard line. Three plays and only four yards later, the Valley Forge punter stood poised to launch another punt.

Coach Smith took a chance and called "Double cross smash," which told Jeff and the player lining up next to him, Joey Lincoln, that they were going to try to block the kick. From his position over the tight end, Jeff ripped across to the outside of the end's face, opening a gap for Lincoln to slice through inside of him on a clear path to the punter. The play worked to perfection. Lincoln dove headlong and took the ball right off the punter's foot. The ball rolled backwards towards the Warrior goal line where it was fallen on by Mike Mattingly, the Hillmen's 300 lb. defensive tackle on the eight yard line.

Two plays later, Lewis scored again, this time on a sweep around the right side, led by a crushing block on the cornerback by fullback Lipinski. The crowd was now in a frenzy, since, even though the PAT failed again, Hillsdale had taken the lead for the first time 12-7 as the fourth quarter got underway.

Players from both sides really got into the game now as the battle for field position continued. After an exchange of punts, Valley Forge found itself with the ball on its thirty-three yard line with just over four minutes to go. The first play after the change of possession was a fade pass to their 6' 3" split end who had been held in check by Lewis most of the game. As the ball sailed down the sideline, Lewis and the Warrior receiver were running neck and neck, when, all of a sudden, free safety Jeremy Johnson appeared from nowhere to make a play on the ball. The trio went up at the highest point, but Johnson inadvertently knocked Lewis out of position. The threesome tumbled to the ground, and the ball landed on the lap of the Valley Forge end for a gain of thirty yards, down to the Hillmen thirty-four yard line.

Lewis got up angrily from the play because he felt he would have picked off the pass had not Johnson ran into him. Johnson didn't get up at all. The senior safety had injured his knee and had to be helped off the field. Jerry Smith knew whom to call on. "Fairchild! Get in there!"

For the first time in the second half, Valley Forge had gotten a break, and momentum seemed to shift their way. Bubba Brown was a wild man in the stands, exhorting his Maroon and White squad to finish the job. The Warrior offense snapped out of the huddle and made its move to try and score the winning touchdown.

The Hillsdale Hillmen defense had other ideas. With the game on the line and a new vocal leader on the field in Jeff Fairchild, Hillsdale gave ground grudgingly, forcing the Warriors to use up almost two minutes to gain a first down. With the ball on the Hillmen twenty-two yard line and less than two minutes to play, Coach Jim Buchanan called his second time out of the half.

The Valley Forge offense huddled around its head coach to plan the final strategy. But to Bubba, the plan was simple. "Get the ball to Brown!" he screamed. "Get the ball to Brad! Twenty-five! Twenty-five! Get the ball to Twenty-Five." Helen wasn't quite as loud, but she joined in with the rest of the Valley Forge cheering section.

After a short gain and with the clock running, it looked like Bubba was going to get his wish. Brad Brown headed towards left tackle. But it was a fake, and the entire defense of Hillsdale was fooled. The Warrior quarterback rolled out to his right on a bootleg and hit the tight end in the flat with a short toss. The big receiver rumbled down the far sideline in front of the Valley Forge crowd who roared its approval. Before he was knocked out of bounds, he had traveled all the way to the eight yard line. Valley Forge had the ball. First and goal to go.

August 26 --- Game Day

Chapter 59

The clock read 1:33. Valley Forge had only one timeout left. The game was in the hands of the Hillsdale defense, and behind the fence just to the north of that end zone, one former coach was sweating bullets. Never before had Ben Reynolds felt so helpless. Rather than yell and scream like all of the people around him, he narrowed his eyes and tried to zero in on the proceedings. From his scouting report, he already knew what formation Jim Buchanan would run—the old-fashioned double tight end T-formation. He also knew that their favorite play out of that formation was a cross buck lead play to their right side.

He knew this because of all the hours he had spent scouting video tape of Buchanan's games and studying tendency charts from his computer. He was so glad that he had advanced to the modern technology; it had saved him and his staff so much time. Since Ben knew this information, he also knew that Jerry Smith was well aware of it as well. That's why he wasn't surprised when Smith took a timeout after the long pass play. He wanted to make sure his Hillmen knew what to expect.

Smith and Reynolds were right on as Buchanan ran the same cross buck play twice in a row for a total of three yards. With third and goal from the five and forty seconds to play, Valley Forge called its final timeout.

Ben Reynolds stood in the end zone and thought amidst the roar around him, "What play will he run now? Who does he trust? Who's his best player? The bootleg got them down there, so that will be the play he runs first. Then it will be Brad Brown on the last play. I hope Jerry is thinking the same way. It has to be that combination. But he could switch them around. Run first and pass second. It has to be those two plays, but in which order?"

Valley Forge came out in the I formation, so Ben at least knew he was on the right track. On a quick count, the ball was pitched to Brown who hot-footed it towards the near sideline. He got a block from his fullback and appeared to have the corner turned, heading towards the winning score. He never saw the hit coming.

From his free safety spot, Jeff Fairchild had a simple read. "Watch the tackle. He will tell me if it's run or pass." By his second step, Jeff knew what was coming. He took a proper angle and attacked the ball carrier as hard as his legs would take him. His facemask hit Brad Brown right on the chest and across onto the ball, just like he had been taught since his freshman year. The ball flew up out of Brown's hands and floated in the air. It hit the ground and a wild scramble ensued. Fairchild scrambled to his feet as fast as he could. No way were they going to let Valley Forge fall onto that ball!

The melee rolled over into the end zone. If a Warrior fell on it, it would be the winning touchdown. Somehow, Fairchild dove into the pile and ended on the bottom. Players were grabbing everything they could, jerseys, legs, facemasks, anything. The officials raced in and began pulling players off the pile. One by one they were tossed off, but Jeff Fairchild was still down on the bottom fighting another Valley Forge player for possession.

Because his hands were so sweaty, Jeff was losing his hold on the ball. The Warrior player was gaining an advantage. Just before the officials reached the bottom, Jeff resorted to a last ditch effort. With all of the strength he could muster, he punched at the ball. On his second try, the squirted through the Warrior player's arms and rolled out of bounds out of the end zone.

The official gave the signal for a touchback and the ball belonged to Hillsdale on it own twenty.

Coach Jim Buchanan was furious. He had run over half-way onto the field in anticipation of the winning score, and when he discovered the result of the play, he flung his hat into the air. He couldn't believe those referees had not allowed his team the winning TD. He wanted a piece of every official on the field. His assistants had to literally drag him off the field. He was kicking and screaming every cuss word under the sun at them. Despite all the efforts to control him, the officials had no recourse except to flag him for Unsportsmanlike Conduct twice and eventually ejected him from the game. It took a police escort to remove him from that ugly scene on the Warrior sideline.

So, once order was restored, Shule took a knee at the twenty-two, and the Hillmen won a memorable game 12-7.

August 26 --- Game Day

Chapter 60

Bubba Brown sat dejectedly in the Valley Forge bleachers. He didn't say a word. For the second game in a row, a fumble by Brad Brown inside the five yard line prevented his team from scoring the winning touchdown. His son. His son who was supposed to get a scholarship playing for Coach Buchanan. His son who moved away from Hillsdale to Valley Forge.

This was not the way Bubba and Helen envisioned it, but she seemed to be more concerned with Brad's feelings, rather than Bubba's. She left her seat and started to head toward the Warrior locker room. Bubba continued to stare out into the field and watch the celebration of the Hillsdale fans, who had stormed the field and were dancing around each other. He wasn't sure but he thought he saw Ben Reynolds right out there in the middle of them. That asshole!

The two teams met in the middle of the field and exchanged pleasantries. Brad was last in the line. He trudged forward and shook hands with some of the younger

Hillmen players who had not seen any action. When he came to the end of the line and the guys who actually played in the game, he hugged each one of them. By the time Jeff Fairchild showed up, a long, lasting embrace occurred. If Bubba hadn't known better, he would have sworn his son was crying.

Brown was the last one out of the bleachers. He decided against going to the Warrior locker room and joining his wife to see Brad. He didn't want to risk running into Buchanan outside and feel his wrath. Shoot, Buchanan probably blamed Bubba for that final mistake.

As he trudged around the fence heading for the gate, Brown didn't notice Joe Josephson and Jason Stone standing together as he passed by. They couldn't resist that final dig, "Hey Bubba! You've had a good week, haven't you?" They broke up in laughter.

Bubba retorted, "Screw you!" and kept on walking.

As he headed towards his truck, he muttered, "You haven't heard the last of me yet."

August 26 --- Game Day

Chapter 61

After the final horn, Ben Reynolds hopped the fence and raced towards the field before Kurt Hayes could stop him. As he bounced out onto the game field, he threw his traditional uppercut punch accompanied by several "Yeahs!" to go along with it. He quickly found Coach Jerry Smith and hugged him before he could cross the field and shake hands with the Valley Forge staff. He congratulated Coach Mays for keeping his head in the game. He head-butted the first four players he saw. He made a special effort to find Jeff Fairchild and lifted him off the ground. He high-fived Kemper Shule and Jake Lewis till his hands stung.

His euphoria was so genuine and real that it seemed like he had been out there on the field all night long. The Hillsdale crowd chanted, "Coach! Coach! Coach!" in full support of their stricken leader.

And just like that, he turned and ran off the field through the crowd and disappeared into the throng of well-wishing fans. He hadn't really wanted to steal the team's thunder, but he just couldn't help himself. It was time for him to go. He jogged all the way to his truck where Kurt Hayes was waiting.

"Let's go celebrate, Ben," he smiled. "I think you deserve it."

August 26 --- Game Day

Chapter 62

It was late, and she was exhausted.

Rachel Sawyer looked at her watch. 11:15. She needed a good night sleep after the night's work she had. The Hillsdale crowd was more than energized when they showed up for "Victory Pie" after that thrilling win. *The Cabin* was definitely hopping. The fans had lots to talk about that night. The "award" given to Mark Lowery. Coach Reynolds showing up. The injuries in the game. The great hitting on both sides (everybody was picking their favorite hit of the game). That crazy last play. Jeff Fairchild, of all people. Who'd think he could make a hit like that?

Some had stayed over an hour, just buzzing about what they had just seen. She was hoping things would quiet down so she could go to the dance at the Moose after the game, but no such luck. All of the thirteen pies that had been baked disappeared in no time. By 10:30, there was nothing left, just drinks. Finally, the final customer went home at 11:00.

It normally didn't take long to clean up, and tonight was no exception. In less than fifteen minutes, the counter was spic and span, and everything was back in its place, waiting for another day tomorrow. The last item on the agenda each night was to wipe off the picture of Ray and Elise before the rags were put into the wash machine. Kind of a good luck, final tribute to the original owners.

When Rachel finished her duties, she gathered her belongings and headed out the back door. The other help who had come in later that night agreed to close up and lock the doors. The light wasn't good in the back as she tried to count her tips for the night. "Looks like close to $100," she thought, as she edged towards her car.

"That's far enough, Rachel," an ominous voice from the shadows said. "Don't move. Don't even breathe."

Rachel spun around. She couldn't see the figure, but she recognized the voice. "What do you want, Mr. Brown?"

Bubba Brown emerged from the shadows by the back door. "Brad needs a little cheering up, Rachel. He's had a rough night, and he needs a little TLC. I thought I would take you to him."

"I'm going home, Mr. Brown," Rachel replied firmly. "I have no desire to see Brad tonight…or any other night for that matter." She turned to leave, but he reached out and squeezed her arm. She writhed in his grip.

"What's the matter, little girl? That hurt?"

Her voice raised a bit. "Leave me alone! Hear me?" She tried to twist free, but he had too strong a hold. She could smell whiskey on his breath.

"You should have known I wasn't going to forget that little episode from a few weeks ago," he grinned, "did you? Tonight's Pay Back Night, Li'l La----"

The back door swung open and one of those late-arriving workers appeared. Jeff Fairchild cracked Bubba Brown in the back of the head with a frying pan. Brown went down face first in a heap and didn't move.

Jeff walked up to Rachel and embraced her. She buried her head in his shoulder. "I was afraid, Jeff. Too afraid to scream. Thank you so much…again." She kissed him on the same cheek she had done before.

"Here," he said, handing her a football jersey. "You forgot this. I gave it to you to wear, not leave behind the counter." He smiled and then reached down to kiss her gently on the lips.

Somewhere Ray and Elise Johnson…and Jeff's dad were smiling.

August 26 --- Game Day

Chapter 63

Rocco' Rocks...11:30 p.m. Notes from Hillsdale-Valley Forge

If my first game of the season is any indication of what lies ahead this high school football season, then we are all in for a lot of fun. What a game! Two teams who went after each other from the opening whistle.

Our "Friends of High School Award" had a strange twist. When Mark Lowery learned about all of these reasons he won the honor, he took off running...Strange, but sometimes people get what they deserve...

Hillsdale deserves a lot of credit rallying around their suspended coach Ben Reynolds (who got a raw deal)-Coach Jerry Smith did a great job in a short time in getting that team ready to play...Coach Reynolds was at the game, standing along the fence in the north end zone...when the game ended, he was hootin' and hollerin' like the rest of the crowd...

Valley Forge played their hearts out.....I felt a little sorry for Brad Brown...he was a marked man all night...

that fumble on the goal line...he shouldn't feel bad about that—only a great hit by Jeff Fairchild kept him from being a hero...Brown will be one of the best in the area

How about the temper tantrum by Coach Buchanan... He looked like he had really lost it...heard rumors after the game that he punched out the windows of the team bus... don't know for sure....

How about Jeff Fairchild...came off the bench to make a game-saving tackle...in games like this, it's sometimes the unlikely hero

Finally, the food at Hillsdale lived up to its expectations... those pork chops added five pounds to my mid-section..... well worth the trip if you are in the area...A great first week......lookin' forward to seein' ya down the road.

Rocco

August 27

Epilogue

The hot August night had cooled down considerably. A bright moon shone overhead. Julie and Ben Reynolds stood at the fifty yard line of the high school field. They had been walking back and forth up and down the field for over half an hour. The only other lighting was the series of nightlights splattered around the all-weather track to aid nighttime walkers or joggers. Tonight the track was vacant as the Hillsdale fans were still out celebrating this big win.

Julie and Ben met at Jerry Smith's house after the game for that long-awaited party Jerry was supposed to host. They only stayed for an hour, since they wanted Jerry and the current staff to enjoy the moment without any more undue attention to him and his plight.

Surprisingly, it was Ben's idea to take this walk. Julie was more than willing to do anything to cheer her husband up, although she knew the game that night had done some good.

They had walked in silence for some time, holding hands, when they came to a halt in the middle of the field.

"Look," Julie spoke. "Police lights over at *The Cabin*. Wonder if they had a break-in or something."

Ben looked at his watch. "Too late for a fight. They've been closed for over an hour. Hope it ain't nothing big."

Julie turned to her husband and put her hand on his shoulder. "Why'd you want to come here tonight, Ben?"

He spoke slowly and deliberately. "I like it here. Next to our house, I guess this is my home. I never knew.... how much it meant to me until tonight. I... like it here."

"But you know you can't be here this year."

"Yeah, I know. That'll be hard. Real hard. It's like in *Field of Dreams*. I'm gonna need something to 'ease my pain.' Walkin' this field eases my pain."

They edged towards the Hillsdale sideline. Ben dragged his feet along the way.

"You should coach next year, Ben. You're not ready to give this up."

"You may be right. But I don't know. Would it be the right move for me? Or should I just..."

Julie cut him off. "Look at you. Look at you tonight. You were nuts out here after the game. I didn't know whether to laugh, cheer for you, or just hit you over the head."

He chuckled, "That's what being in this sport for all these years has made me."

They finally stopped in the north end zone. Ben looked into Julie's eyes.

"Ben, you're a coach. You're one today; you'll be one tomorrow. No Monty Phillips or any State ruling can change who you are. They may take the title away; they may make you sit on the sideline this year, but they can't take away your spirit or your passion. Once a coach, always a coach."

Ben smiled. "You're the second person to tell me that tonight."

"Just do me a favor."

"What's that?"

"No more DVDs at *The Cabin*."

The coach and his wife held a long embrace under the moonlight sky. In the distance, the flashing lights at *The Cabin* flickered above their silhouette.

About the Author

 Mick Peterson resides in Pontiac, Illinois, with his wife Carole and his daughter Emily. They are also parents of Katie (Dr. Bryan) Huff, Julie, and Drew. Mick received his bachelor's degree from Augustana (IL) College and his Master's degree from Illinois State University. After thirty-four years as a high school teacher and coach, he plans to retire after the 2008 school year. He began his career at Flora High School (1974-84) where he taught English and was an assistant coach in both football and basketball. In 1984, he moved to Walnut (IL) High School, where he taught both English and PE and served as head football coach, assistant boys basketball coach, and head girls track coach. His football teams in Walnut won four conference championships and advanced to quarterfinal round in the Class 1A State Tournament in each of his five years at the helm, compiling an overall record of 50-9. Mick and his family finally settled in Pontiac in 1989, where he has been a member of both the PE and, more recently, the English departments for the past nineteen years. He served as the head football coach for

eighteen years, assistant boys basketball coach for four years, assistant girls track coach for five years and head girls track coach for eleven years. During his tenure as head football coach, his squads won ten conference championships and qualified for the State playoffs on fifteen different occasions. Twice Pontiac reached the semi-final round, and in 1993, they captured the Class 3A championship. After the 2006 season, he retired from coaching with an overall record at Pontiac of 136-47.

Mick had articles published in various coaching magazines throughout his career, and he has been responsible for publishing a bi-monthly church newsletter, but this is his first attempt at a novel.

Printed in the United States
97515LV00001B/1-99/A